"Are You Going To Demand That I Tear Off My Clothes So That You Can Have Your Wicked Way With Me?" William Asked.

Now *that* idea had possibilities, Bailey thought. She met William's gaze as she scrambled to find a snappy retort, all in the name of fun.

But her breath caught as she realized that William was no longer smiling. The merriment that had shown in his expressive gray eyes had changed into a blatant message of desire.

His playful suggestion had obviously moved into an arena of reality in his mind and, heaven help her, in hers as well.

There were only the two of them, and a want and need like nothing she'd experienced before.

Dear Reader,

As the weather gets cold, cold, cold, Silhouette Desire gets hot, hot, hot! (If you live in Florida, Southern California or some other *warm* place, just imagine us living up north, *freezing!*) Anyway, here at Desire, we're generating *our* heat from six sensuous stories written by six spectacular authors. And they're all here, this month, in our HEAT UP YOUR WINTER collection.

Just take a look at this fabulous line-up: a *Man of the Month* from Lass Small; the next installment in the SOMETHING WILD series by Ann Major; and fantastic stories by Dixie Browning, Barbara Boswell, Mary Lynn Baxter and Robin Elliott. And I'm sure you've already noticed that this is one of our now-famous MONTHS OF MEN, with six sinfully sexy hero portraits on the front covers. (Aren't these guys *cute?*)

At Silhouette Desire we're dedicated to bringing you the very best short, sexy books around. Let us know—do you think we're succeeding? Are the books *too* sexy? Could you stand some more sizzle? Or maybe you think they're "just right." Write me! I'm here to listen.

In the meantime, HEAT UP YOUR WINTER with Silhouette Desire.

All the best,

Lucia Macro
Senior Editor

ROBIN ELLIOTT

NOT JUST ANOTHER PERFECT WIFE

SILHOUETTE *Desire®*

Published by Silhouette Books

America's Publisher of Contemporary Romance

SILHOUETTE BOOKS

ISBN 0-373-05818-7

NOT JUST ANOTHER PERFECT WIFE

ROBIN ELLIOTT

lives in a small, charming town in the high pine country of Arizona. She enjoys watching football, attending craft shows on the town square and gardening. Robin has published over sixty novels and also writes under her own name, Joan Elliott Pickart.

For the Admiral,
with love and the deepest admiration.
Thank you, Phil.

One

It was raining on her bonbons.

Bailey Crandell lifted the cardboard box from the lowered tailgate of the station wagon, then glowered up at the dark clouds. The rain that had begun to fall as she drove across town was the lazy, misty kind that was very common in August in Phoenix, during the last of the monsoon season.

No thunder rumbled, nor did jagged streaks of lightning shoot across the sky. It was a quiet summer rain that might have enticed her to sit by a window and watch, the gentle fall easing tension and stress.

It was Bailey's favorite type of rainfall, and normally she would have thoroughly enjoyed it.

But not today.

Because it was raining on her bonbons.

"Blast," she muttered.

She hefted the box higher and hugged it to her chest as she backed away from the car. Her pink cotton blouse and flowered wraparound skirt were quickly becoming soaked, and she could feel her hair being plastered to her head.

She even had wet toes, for Pete's sake, due to the flat strappy sandals she wore.

The cardboard box was getting wetter by the minute, and the jars and tins of bonbons, sour balls, peppermint sticks, pralines and chocolate-covered raisins inside were drenched. The rain played an off-key tune on the metal lids of the jars and tins, the sound grating further on Bailey's nerves.

Mumbling an unladylike word, she turned with the intention of crossing the parking lot to enter the building beyond. At the exact moment, a white van appeared directly in front of her, the tires hitting the numerous puddles and creating a heavy spray of muddy water that covered Bailey from head to toe.

"Aaak!" she shrieked.

The driver of the van slammed on the brakes, the far door was flung open, and a man came barreling around the front of the vehicle to where Bailey stood.

"What's wrong?" he yelled. "I heard you scream. Did I hit you?"

Fury bubbled up in Bailey, to the point that she could feel the flush of its heat on her wet, muddy cheeks. Clutching the soggy box even tighter, she turned to face the man, vaguely registering the fact that he was very tall and had broad shoulders.

Beyond that, she really didn't care what he looked like, or who he was. She would gladly have strangled him with her bare hands.

"I screamed, you giant-size idiot," she said, her words slow and measured, "because you soaked me completely through with muddy water. Lots of muddy water. Extremely muddy muddy water."

"Oh," he said, his gaze flickering over her. "Is that all? Lord, I thought I'd creamed you from the way you cut loose."

"Is that *all?*" she hollered. The man cringed. "Look at me. I'm a mess."

"Not really. I mean, the rain is doing an adequate job of washing you off. You do realize that I'm now wet to the skin from standing here talking to you, don't you?"

"Oh, that does it. That's it. Get out of my way." She started to walk around him. "Aaak!" she cried again in the next instant.

"Would you stop doing that? Lord, you've got the lungs of a fullback."

"Do something! The entire bottom of this box is letting go!"

The man said something under his breath that Bailey didn't quite hear but decided she could live without asking to be repeated. He moved in front of her and slid his hands under the box, then up the other side, his fingers brushing against her breasts.

With the bottom of the box resting on his forearms, he stopped, the backs of his hands on her breasts. He was bent over, his gaze meeting hers.

Gray eyes, Bailey thought hazily. He had warm gray eyes, pussy-willow gray, fuzzy kitten gray. And before it had been plastered to his head by the rain, she'd cataloged the information that his hair was thick, and dark as night.

His features were rugged, rough-hewn enough to transform mere handsomeness into masculinity personified. Long, dark eyelashes framed those incredible gray eyes. He looked vaguely familiar, although she knew that if she'd met him before she'd most definitely remember.

Bailey, she admonished herself, *pay attention.* This man, this stranger, had his hands against her breasts. The pressure was causing a frisson of heat to slither down her back, then weave into a thrumming coil deep within her.

The whole scenario was bizarre. There she stood, she realized, pinned in place by mesmerizing gray eyes, wet and muddy, about to lose her precious bonbons through the bottom of the rain-soaked box, with a total stranger's hands resting against her breasts. Breasts that were beginning to feel heavy and achy from the sensuous sensation.

Enough was enough.

"Bonbons," she said, hearing the shaky quality of her voice.

"Who?" he said, his voice gritty.

"The bonbons are in tins that will be dented, and the jars are going to be smashed to smithereens if they fall through the bottom of the box."

"Oh, yeah, right . . ."

He lifted the carton from her arms and held it tightly to his chest.

"Got it." He paused. "Look, I'm sorry I splashed you with muddy water. I just didn't see you."

"Well, this wet weather isn't your fault. I apologize for scaring you to death by screaming like that."

He smiled then, and Bailey's heart seemed to do a strange little flip-flop.

"I'm William Lansing," he said.

Bailey returned his smile. "Hello, William Lansing. I'm Bailey Crandell."

Bailey, William repeated silently. The name was unique, unusual, had a fun sound to it. It suited her. Even soaking-wet, Bailey Crandell was attractive, with delicate features and big blue eyes.

She was about five foot four, and her hair was short. He couldn't be certain at this point what color it was. It was slicked down and dripping water and the effect accentuated the summer-sky blue of her eyes.

"Well, Bailey," he said, "how about pretending we have enough sense to come in out of the rain?" He glanced up. "I'd better move my van before someone drives into the lot and plows right into me."

"I'll take the box."

"No, I'll slide it into the seat of the van, then tote it inside. I presume you're taking part in this bazaar that my sister conned us all into."

"Alice is your sister? No wonder I thought you looked familiar. There's a definite family resemblance." She laughed. "Yes, I'm taking part in the bazaar. Your sister can be very persuasive."

"My sister," he said, chuckling, "can be a pain in the neck. Her husband, Raymond—poor guy—has his hands full being married to Alice Lansing Wilson. So, let's go in and get out of the rain. I'll see you inside."

"Yes."

They stood there in the rain for another moment, smiling at each other, both of them seeming strangely reluctant to be on their way. Then they both moved at once, suddenly hurrying as though the rain had just started and they were attempting to stay as dry as possible.

Bailey went back to her car and lifted another box from the station wagon, balancing it on one arm as she closed the tailgate. She rushed toward the brick building.

William sat behind the wheel of the van and watched her go.

Bailey Crandell, he mused. She'd had an impact on him, no doubt about it. He'd felt, could still feel, the heated tightening low in his body. The onslaught of the rain had not had the effect of a cold shower, that was for sure.

He glanced at the jars and tins in the soggy box next to him on the seat.

Bailey Crandell, who owned Sweet Fantasy, he thought. He'd heard Alice singing the praises of the delicious candy offered at her friend's store.

According to Alice, Sweet Fantasy was gaining popularity at a steady, profitable rate. He'd tasted several of its selections while at Alice's, and had agreed that they were excellent.

William turned the key in the ignition and drove into a parking slot.

So, that was Miss Sweet Fantasy, he mentally went on. She was a successful career woman, and he respected the hard work and dedication he knew it must have taken for her to achieve her goal. She appeared to be about twenty-five or twenty-six, which was young to have accomplished what she had.

William frowned as he took the key from the ignition.

Yes, Bailey must be an extremely focused career woman. Well, he'd like to get to know her better, test the waters to see if she was interested in some casual dates.

If she was unattached, there was no harm in having some pleasant outings with her, as long as he didn't lose sight of the fact that nothing would ever come of it.

For as long as he could remember, he'd known what type of woman he wanted to marry and spend the remainder of his life with. In a nutshell—old-fashioned. He would be the provider, she the nurturer. The focal point of her existence would be him, their children, their home.

Mrs. Old-Fashioned would be there when the kids came in from school. She'd share milk and cookies—made-from-scratch cookies—hear about their day, praise them or comfort them, depending on their needs. She would be genuinely happy in a world of hearth and home, rather than an uptown world of business lunches and power suits.

And at the center of her universe would be her husband, him, William Lansing.

An old-fashioned woman, he thought, then sighed. A woman from another era, back in time—an endangered species, to say the least. The fact that he was thirty-five years old and hadn't yet found her testified to the fact that women of the old school were not waiting around every corner.

Whenever he'd presented his outlook to a woman he was dating, sort of tested the waters, he'd received negative reactions in a vast range of intensity.

That fact was frustrating and disappointing. It wasn't as though he felt it took less ability, intelligence, motivation—on and on the list went—to fulfill the role he was describing than to be a successful career woman.

The truth of the matter was, he saw the old-fashioned woman—The Perfect Wife, as he referred to her in his mind—as facing a tremendously demanding and difficult challenge. The title "household executive" was appropriate and well-deserved, and he would highly respect any woman capable of performing in that capacity.

But even with that attitude, his philosophy was not well received by the females who crossed his path. It was, to say the least, discouraging.

William frowned, shook his head, then opened the door of the van and reluctantly moved once again into the steady stream of rain.

Inside the building, Bailey swept her gaze over the large expanse, where fifty people or more were creating what appeared to be total chaos.

The noise level was high, and she wondered who was listening to whom, since it seemed as though everyone were talking.

Rows of tables had been set up and covered with crepe paper in a multitude of bright colors. People were scurrying around, giving the impression that mass confusion was the order of the day, yet smiles were everywhere, and there was an upbeat, festive mood in the air.

"Hi," a voice said.

Bailey turned to see a young woman seated behind a card table.

"I'm Sheila, and you're soaking wet."

Bailey laughed. "I am indeed. Drenched to the skin, as a matter of fact."

"Well, don't feel alone," Sheila said cheerfully. "There are oodles of soggy folks in here. If you give me your name, I'll tell you where your table is."

Minutes later, Bailey located her designated spot and begun to unpack the contents of the box. Each jar and tin boasted a label with a pale blue background dotted with fluffy clouds. Through the clouds flew Pegasus.

The containers held treasures to tempt even the most difficult to please—chocolate-covered cherries, pretzels dipped in white chocolate, gumdrops, licorice straws, jelly beans, caramel-pecan Turtles, sinfully rich fudge and more.

She had just placed the last tin on the table when William arrived.

"Delivery service," he said. He set the wet box on the floor behind Bailey's table.

Before she could reply, an attractive woman in her late thirties appeared from the opposite direction.

"You both made it," she said. "That's great. Isn't this fun?"

"A thrill a minute," William said dryly. "I always enjoy spending a day in wet, clammy clothes. You *are* going to tell me there isn't time to go home and change, aren't you, Alice?"

"I certainly am. William have you met Bailey?"

"Yes, we met in the parking lot."

"Good," Alice said. "Bailey, you really are wet. I'm sorry about the weather, but at least it's warm, so no one should catch a chill."

"I'll dry out," Bailey said. "Don't worry about it, Alice."

"If I come down with a cold, dear sister," William said, "you're doing the juice-and-chicken-soup routine until I'm hale and hearty again."

"William, don't be a grump," Alice said. "This bazaar is for a good cause."

"We've heard it, Alice, we've heard it," William said, laughing. "This is the Golden Years Retirement Village. This building—" he swept one arm in the air, "—is the activity center. This bazaar is to raise funds for supplies needed to enable these folks to make crafts, which they in turn will sell at—"

"Their own bazaars in the future," Bailey finished for him, then burst out laughing.

"Okay, okay," Alice said, raising both hands. "So I had my spiel down pat. It got you both here, didn't it?" She paused. "William, you haven't even set up your table yet. We're opening the doors to the public in fifteen minutes. Shoo! Go get the pots of herbs you promised to donate to sell. And, yes, the fact that you grew those herbs with your own little hands is duly noted with awe and wonder. Go, go..."

"Lord you're a nag," William said. "How does Raymond put up with you?"

"He loves me. Now go!"

William spun around and strode away. Bailey watched him leave, then glanced up to see Alice watching her and watching William.

"Handsome devil, isn't he?" Alice said, leaning slightly toward Bailey. "He's intelligent, too, and thoughtful, hardworking—"

Bailey interrupted her, smiling, "And brave, coura-geous and bold? Alice, please, no matchmaking."

Alice sighed. "Matchmaking can be very produc-tive, but in this case I'd be wasting my time. You and William are totally wrong for each other."

"Why? Not that I approve of matchmaking, but why would you say we're wrong for each other?"

"Because William is searching for an old-fashioned woman, one who would devote herself to hearth, home, husband and babies. You and I have chatted enough since we met for me to know that your first priority is your shop. William has stood firm in his determination to find that old-fashioned woman for more years than I can remember. So..." She shrugged. "You two are wrong for each other."

"Oh," Bailey said, looking in the direction William had gone. "I see. He's a bit out of step with the times, wouldn't you say?"

"Yes, but try telling *him* that. Well, I must make my rounds. This place is a zoo. Get your table set up, Bai-ley, because everything starts in a few minutes."

"I'll be ready."

Alice hurried away, and Bailey picked up a jar of sour balls from the box on the floor. But before she put it on the table, her hand stilled as she once again stared in the direction William had gone.

How strange, she thought. The announcement that she was the wrong woman for William Lansing had caused a gloomy feeling to settle over her, as though one of the ominous dark clouds from outside had materialized directly above her.

That was ridiculous. If William was determined to find an old-fashioned woman who centered her emotional and physical energies entirely on her husband, her home and her children, then she was indeed the wrong woman for him.

Sweet Fantasy came first in her life. It was an extension of her, of who she was. She was a career woman determined to make a success of her own business, and nothing would lure her from the path she now traveled.

She knew what sacrifices were necessary to achieve her goal. She dated occasionally, when time allowed, but there was no room in her life for a serious relationship. Daydreams of a loving husband and a baby created with that man had long ago been pushed into a dusty corner of her mind. She just couldn't have it all. She'd made her choice. So be it.

Then why this sudden case of the blues? she wondered. Yes, William Lansing was a ruggedly handsome and extremely masculine man. He exuded an aura of blatant all-male sexuality, and he'd seemed to cast a sensuous spell over her when he pinned her in place with those marvelous gray eyes.

But that was not just cause to feel this sense of disappointment upon learning that she and William were poles apart in what they wanted on the personal plane.

So, fine. She knew her reaction to what Alice had said was absurd. Therefore, she was dismissing it, declaring it irrational, not worthy of further thought. That was that. The end of the nonsense.

With a decisive nod, Bailey thudded the jar of sour balls down on the table, then unloaded the remainder of the box. She was arranging the tins and jars into an attractive display when William reappeared. He was carrying an enormous open-topped carton that he set on the floor behind the table next to hers.

"Hi, neighbor," he said, glancing over at her. "It stopped raining out there. Now that we're both wet to the skin, the sun is beginning to shine."

Bailey laughed. "That figures. Well, at least there's a better chance of people coming to the bazaar. I'm drying out quite a bit already."

William turned to look directly at her. "I told you the rain had washed away the mud I splashed on you. You're as good as new."

Ebony, he mused. Her hair was shiny ebony, and framed her face with short, soft curls. His fingers were actually tingling from the urge to weave them through the silky waves. Lord, she was beautiful. She wasn't knock-'em-dead stunning, with big-city flash. No, hers was a fresh, wholesome, pretty-as-a-picture beauty.

"William?" Bailey said, cocking her head. "Is something wrong? You're staring at me with a very strange expression on your face."

"What? Oh, no, nothing's wrong. Not at all. I was just thinking about something. Well, I'd better get organized before Alice the Hun shows up again."

As William busied himself with the task at hand, Bailey fiddled and fussed with her display, stealing glances at William from beneath her lashes in the process.

He was wearing snug black jeans that accentuated his long, muscular legs and his nice, *nice* tush. His knit shirt was royal blue, and the color did wonderful things for his tan, his gray eyes, and his rich, dark hair.

She really liked his voice, Bailey mused, and she liked the sound of his laughter and the way his eyes crinkled at the corners when he smiled.

That's great, Bailey, she admonished herself. What was next? She'd gaze longingly at him, sigh deeply, then dissolve into a puddle at his feet? Her reaction to William was so adolescent, it was a crime. She had to take herself in hand before she made a complete fool of herself.

"There," William said, causing Bailey to jerk as his voice jarred her from her thoughts. "That's as good as it gets."

She turned to look at his display, smiling in approval. The table held a wide selection of herbs in a multitude of colored plastic pots. The effect was bright and cheerful, and the herbs were obviously healthy and well tended.

"Lovely," she said. "You grew them?"

"I certainly did, ma'am. I've never attempted to play gardener before, and I'm getting a kick out of it. I've decided to increase my selection of herbs, which means back to the library to study some more." He sat down on the metal folding chair behind his table. He frowned and shook his head. "This is not how I planned to spend my Saturday. But—" he shrugged, "—Alice had me wrapped around her little finger from the day I was born. There's no reason to believe that's ever going to change. Where did you meet her?"

Bailey settled on her own chair. "At aerobics class, about a year ago. I've seen her two mornings a week ever since, and we've become friends. We fit in a lunch together from time to time, and she comes to my store, Sweet Fantasy, quite often."

"I imagine Sweet Fantasy keeps you very busy."

"Very," she said, nodding.

"I've had the pleasure of sampling some of your candies at Alice's. They were delicious."

"Thank you, sir," she said, dipping her head slightly. "We aim to please."

"Now that I think about it, I'd heard of your place before Alice told me. You have an excellent reputation. I'm impressed."

Bailey smiled, searching her mind for something to say other than a mundane "Thank you." There was nothing within her reach, she discovered. She also discovered to her surprise, that she was basking in William's praise and that his words caused a warm, glowy feeling within her.

She'd had compliments from other men regarding her business, the success she'd achieved in just over three years. Praise was always pleasant to hear, but she couldn't remember ever reacting to the degree she was now to William's flattery.

Dumb, she told herself. She was sitting there like a dolt, relishing the idea that she'd just gone up a notch or two in William's eyes.

What she'd do well to remember was that the most important item on William Lansing's checklist for a woman was her stand on devoting herself to hearth, home, husband and babies. He wanted an old-fashioned girl, not a modern, career-oriented woman of the nineties.

Why on earth was she wasting her time thinking about what William wanted? Her mind was trekking down a road she knew was not hers to travel. There was no room in her life, no space, no time, for a serious relationship, a commitment to a man that would require emotional and physical energy.

It had been a conscious and well-thought-out decision on her part. Sweet Fantasy was, and would remain, her number one priority, with everything else fitted in around the edges when possible.

Get it together, Bailey Crandell, she told herself. She'd view William as she did all the other men who appeared in her life. There were those she would consider sharing casual dates with, and there were those who didn't interest her in the least.

William Lansing definitely interested her.

For an occasional outing, she tacked on quickly. That was it, nothing more. If he asked her out, she'd go. If he didn't, it was no big deal. Or, what the heck, *she* might invite *him* to share dinner and a movie.

Right? Right.

Two

For the next hour, as people began to arrive to shop at the bazaar, Bailey was kept busy. The noise level in the building was increasing, but despite the roar of talk and laughter, she was aware that William had sneezed close to a dozen times.

She'd glanced over at him often to see him talking with those who stopped at his table. Much to her disgust, she'd felt a flutter in the pit of her stomach whenever that dazzling smile of his appeared on his tanned, handsome face.

At noon, Alice rushed up, deposited soft drinks and cellophane-wrapped sandwiches on Bailey's and William's tables, said "Bless you" when William sneezed, then whizzed off again.

"She's exhausting to watch," Bailey said laughing. She unwrapped her sandwich and took a bite, welcoming the noon lull.

William popped the last of one of the halves of his sandwich in his mouth, then took a drink. "When Alice does something," he said, "she gives it her all. One of the organizations she belongs to donated some trees to this place. Alice was right in there digging the holes and helping plant the things. She started coming here on a regular basis to visit, chat, take someone to the doctor, whatever was needed. She became fond of a lot of the elderly folks who live here. When she learned there was a funding problem, her pet project became setting things to rights."

"Commendable. I realized that she was determined that this bazaar be a success, but I guess we never discussed how she became involved."

"Well, she— Achoo! Excuse me."

"William," Bailey said, leaning slightly toward him. "are you catching a cold?"

"Never happen. I haven't had a cold since I was a little kid. Achoo! Achoo! Well, damn!"

"You're catching a cold," Bailey said with a decisive nod.

"I am not!"

"There's no need to get hostile. I mean, everyone catches cold occasionally."

"*I* don't."

"Oh, good grief," she said, smiling. "Forget I mentioned it. I'm obviously stepping on sensitive macho toes."

"Mmm . . ." he said, glaring at her. Then he directed his attention to the other half of his sandwich.

"Well, hello, children," a voice said. "How nice of you to come. Isn't this an exciting day?"

Bailey and William got to their feet, and both were rendered momentarily speechless as their gaze swept over the diminutive woman standing before them.

She was at least seventy years old, and she wore a dark, conservative paisley print dress and a small strand of pearls. Her makeup consisted of nothing more than a trace of pale pink lipstick.

It was the hat perched on top of her curly gray hair that caused Bailey's and William's mouths to drop open. The creation was enormous, giving the tiny woman an unbalanced, top-heavy appearance.

The entire surface of the straw hat was covered in life-size plastic fruit—a banana, a green apple, a bunch of purple grapes, a cluster of red cherries and an orange, complete with stems and an abundance of bright green leaves.

"I'm Mary Margaret Swan," the woman said, beaming. "I live here at Golden Years. Isn't that a delightful name for this place?" She laughed. The sound was merry and infectious, and it caused both Bailey and William to smile.

"And who are you, children?" Mary Margaret asked.

William made the introductions, then said, "I really like your hat."

"Isn't it spectacular?" She gave it a pat. "It weighs a tad more than I'd prefer, but it's so unique, utterly smashing, that I wear it more often than not. Alice says it suits me to a T."

"Alice is William's sister," Bailey said.

"Oh?" Mary Margaret said. She squinted and leaned toward William, her hat sliding precariously forward. She used both hands to hold on to the fruity creation. "Yes. I can see the family resemblance. You're definitely Alice's brother, dear."

William laughed. "That's comforting to know, Mary Margaret, because that's who I thought I was."

"It's always a relief to discover you are who you believe yourself to be, isn't it?" Mary Margaret said. "I'm delighted that I could put your mind at ease, William. During the last year of his life, my dear departed husband, Jeremiah, thought he was Teddy Roosevelt. He was forever blowing his bugle and causing all kinds of mischief, bless his heart."

"He was fortunate to have you as his life's partner," William said.

William was being so patient and kind, Bailey mused. Here was yet another side to him. The man just got better and better.

"Oh, dear," Mary Margaret said, bringing Bailey from her thoughts, "my beautiful hat is starting to give me a headache. I do so want to see everything that's on display here. My room is way on the other side of the grounds, and I'll use up my energy if I trek over there."

"Well . . ." Bailey began.

"Silly me," Mary Margaret chattered on. "I wouldn't trust the care of my hat to just anyone, but you're Alice's brother. Perfect."

With that, she whipped off the huge hat, causing the fruit to wiggle and bounce. She thrust the creation at William, who grabbed it in both hands, by reflex.

"That's better," Mary Margaret said, patting the top of her head. "I'm off to snoop. Thank you, dear, for tending to my hat. It's my most precious and prized possession, but I'm confident that you'll treat it as though it were your own."

"Wait a minute," William said, staring at the hat.

"Of course he will," Bailey interjected. "Anyone passing by will assume that the hat is his due to his special care of it."

"Splendid," Mary Margaret said as she scurried away.

"Hey, whoa, wait!" William said. He held the hat away from him, as though he were afraid it might attack him at any second.

A woman in a short skirt and a tight string sweater sauntered by. "Love your bonnet, babe," she said in a sultry voice. She winked at William before moving on down the row of tables.

"Wonderful," William said, rolling his eyes heavenward. "Just wonderful."

Bailey laughed.

Her feminine-instinct inner voice was broadcasting loud and clear the message that William was not finding the situation all that humorous, and for her to laugh was courting trouble.

But she simply couldn't control her amusement. William seemed frozen in place, staring at the hat with an expression of horror.

Bailey laughed and laughed, and finally sank onto her chair, her arms wrapped around her stomach. She gasped for breath, giving herself a mental shake and a firm directive to quiet down before William strangled her.

But when she glanced up again and saw the murderous expression on William's face, she fell apart, laughing until tears trickled down her cheeks.

Alice came rushing up, halting so quickly that she teetered for a moment. Her eyes widened as she took in the scene before her.

"Oh, good grief," she said, "Mary Margaret has been here. She's a darling, but she has this thing about that hat. The mayor visited here once and ended up holding the awful thing. He never came again, that's for sure. William, it isn't going to explode. Just set it carefully on the floor." She laughed. "Bailey, would you kindly put a cork in it? If you get me started laughing, I won't be able to stop."

"I'm trying," Bailey said, wiping tears of merriment from her cheeks. "But, Alice, it's just so funny. I promise I won't start laughing again." She giggled. "I hope."

William glared at them both, then put the hat beneath his table.

"I wish I had a picture of you holding that thing," Alice said.

Bailey started to laugh.

"Don't you get going again," William said, pointing a finger at her.

Bailey raised both hands in a gesture of truce, and batted her eyelashes.

"I'm not laughing, William. This is a sober, somber expression you see on this face."

"Mmm..." he said, glowering.

"You're a grouch, William Lansing," Alice said, then burst into laughter. "Oh, wait until I tell Raymond about this. He's going to love it. The mighty business tycoon and investment broker extraordinaire, William Lansing, and his glorious hat were seen at the bazaar at—"

"Give me a break, Alice," William said, interrupting her. "What's your price for keeping your mouth shut?"

Alice placed a fingertip on her chin. "Well, let me think about this," she said, staring into space. "It's going to cost you big-time."

"Do note," Bailey interjected, "that I was also an eyewitness to this fiasco. My silence can be bought, too."

"Oh, really?" William said. A slow smile started to form on his lips, then widened into a very smug, all-male grin. "This could get interesting. What do you propose, Bailey? Are you going to demand that I tear off my clothes so that you can have your wicked way with me?''

Now *that* had possibilities, Bailey thought. Then, in the next moment, she told herself to shut up.

She met William's gaze as she scrambled to find a snappy retort—all in the name of fun, of course.

But her breath caught when she realized that William was no longer smiling. The merriment that had shown in his expressive gray eyes had changed into a blatant message of desire.

His playful sexual suggestion had obviously moved into an arena of reality in his mind—and, heaven help her, in hers, as well. The sudden mental image of William standing before her, his magnificent body naked and aroused, was creating a thrumming heat deep within her, and a warm flush on her cheeks.

She told herself to tear her gaze from William's but the command was ignored, and she remained pinned in place. The sights and sounds surrounding her dimmed. It seemed as if a hazy, sensuous mist were swirling around her and William. There was only the two of them, and a want and need like nothing she had ever before experienced.

William was vaguely aware of a trickle of sweat running down his back as he looked at Bailey.

What was going on here? he asked himself. He'd been kidding, going along with the lighthearted banter between Bailey, Alice and himself. But now? The shifting pictures in his mind, of him removing his clothes and

Bailey's, reaching for her, covering her mouth with his, then the two of them tumbling into a bed to mesh their bodies, become one entity, was causing a tightening coil of heat to twist and turn low in his aching body.

Lord, he thought, what was this woman doing to him?

"I...um..." Alice began, then stopped. Her eyes darted back and forth between Bailey and William. She took a step backward. "I'd better go make my rounds, see that everything is running smoothly."

Bailey blinked, the sound of Alice's voice finally penetrating the sensual mist. She turned her head to look at her.

"Pardon me?" Bailey said, her voice sounding strange to her own ears.

"What?" William said, frowning as he looked at his sister.

"Oh, my goodness," Alice said, staring at the pair. She cleared her throat. "Yes, well, I'll check in with you later. Bye." She hurried away.

Bailey began to straighten the jars and tins on her table. She was aware of the trembling of her hands and was angry at herself because of it.

Her reaction to William had been ridiculous, she told herself. And frightening. She was going to ignore him for the remainder of the day, simply pretend that he wasn't there.

"Bailey," William said, his voice low, "before, a few minutes ago—"

Her head snapped up, and she met his gaze.

"No," she said. "It was nothing, William, one of those unexplainable moments out of time that happen with no just cause. It's not worth dwelling on, or blowing out of proportion. It would not, in fact, serve any purpose to even discuss it."

He studied her face for a long moment before speaking. "Right," he said slowly. "I'm going to go find another can of soda. Do you want one?"

She shook her head, and he strode away.

Bailey splayed one hand over her heart and drew a deep—and, she hoped, steadying—breath.

What a performance, she scolded herself. She had, no doubt, presented the very image of a Victorian spinster whose delicate sensibilities would be in a dither if William addressed the issue of the eerie spell that had fallen over them.

Oh, blast, she fumed. She'd overreacted to William, then overreacted to the knowledge that she'd overreacted. And she was confusing her befuddled mind to the point of blowing a mental fuse. Enough was enough. She was once more in control.

"Fine," she said aloud, with a decisive nod.

William retrieved a can of soda from a large ice chest placed against the far wall. He pulled the tab, then realized that he really didn't want the drink.

What he had wanted was to put distance between himself and Bailey. And he had nearly fallen over his own feet to accomplish that goal.

Bailey Crandell, he mused, staring into space. Miss Sweet Fantasy Crandell. She'd thrown him totally off kilter, and the fact that Bailey had adamantly refused to discuss the strange, sensual spell was proof positive that she'd been aware of the eerie scene and had been as jangled by it as he.

William rolled the soda can back and forth between his palms, a frown knitting his brows.

So now what? The episode with Bailey had been one of life's flashing neon signs, demanding attention. Things like that didn't happen for no reason. There had been chemistry present and desire that had increased with every passing second.

So now what? he asked himself again. So now... nothing. What had transpired should, could, and would, be ignored. His initial impulse to pursue it, to discover what it meant, had clearly been a mistake. There was no point to examining the situation closer.

Bailey was an independent, career-oriented woman of the nineties. In order to have accomplished what she had with her shop, her focus would have had to be on her thriving business.

Bailey was lovely, and had a terrific sense of humor, as was evidenced by her fit of laughter when he'd been the recipient of Mary Margaret's hideous hat. But Bailey Crandell was as far removed from being an old-fashioned woman as she could get.

Because of the whatever-it-had-been that had taken place between them, he decided, he would forget his earlier intention to determine whether Bailey would be interested in some casual, pleasant outings. He wouldn't see her again after today, and that was that.

But, damn, he thought in the next instant, he *wanted* to see her again.

"William?"

He looked up to find Alice standing before him.

"What is it?" he said gruffly.

"You're glowering at that can of soda as though it were your worst enemy."

William dropped the can into the trash basket next to the ice chest.

"There," he said, still frowning. "Feel better?"

"Goodness, you're grouchy." Alice paused and looked at him intently. "Of course, a man who has been knocked for a loop by a woman might very well be so shook that he'd cover it up with anger."

"I don't know what you're talking about."

"Oh, William, come on. I was there, remember? The attraction between you and Bailey was like a crackling live electric wire. There was a nearly palpable... *something*...sizzling back and forth. You can't deny it, William."

"But I *can* ignore it, which I intend to do."

Alice sighed. "Because Bailey is a career woman and she is not a walking, talking, made-from-scratch-cookies, old-fashioned girl."

"Got it in one."

"I'd like to throttle you, William Lansing. What happened between you and Bailey back there wasn't run-of-the-mill. Are you really going to turn your back on it and pretend it didn't take place?''

"Yes."

"Lord, you're infuriating. You're operating on such a rigid mind-set, it's ridiculous. You haven't allowed one inch for compromise, give-and-take, finding a middle road. Personally, I think you're behaving like a spoiled brat who wants everything his way, or forget it.''

"Are you finished?" William said.

"No."

"Yes, you are, because I'm not listening anymore. Spoiled brat? No way. I'm a man who has gotten in touch with himself, knows what he wants in his life's partner and won't sell himself short by settling for less. I see nothing wrong with that."

"*I* see you running a dangerous risk of growing old alone, William. Alone and lonely. Multitudes of people, including Raymond and me, are happily married, and it would be incredibly sad if you missed out on what we have because you're so stubborn. Something important happened between you and Bailey. Don't you realize that?"

"Give it a rest, Alice. I've got herbs to sell." He walked away, his exit punctuated by two very loud sneezes.

"Darn you, William Lansing," Alice said. She crossed her arms, narrowed her eyes and stared into space, deep in thought.

* * *

The bazaar was scheduled to end at five o'clock, and the last of the shoppers quickly made their purchases as the hour drew near.

Throughout the afternoon, people arrived in a steady, but manageable stream, making it possible for Bailey and William to avoid speaking to each other without either of them being obviously rude.

Bailey's reassurance to herself that she was once again in control was continually undermined by her acute awareness of William's presence only a few feet away.

He was just so *there,* she fumed inwardly. In her peripheral vision she had seen every move he'd made . . . every sexy, all-male move. She'd heard the rich timbre of his voice, an occasional burst of hearty laughter, as well as at least a dozen sneezes.

He was driving her crazy.

A woman purchased Bailey's last jar of sour balls, emptying the table, then also bought two pots of herbs, which was all William had left to sell.

Bailey sank onto her folding chair with a weary sigh, then looked over at William when he sneezed yet again. He was slouched in his chair, one hand covering his face as he squeezed his temples.

"Aren't you feeling well, William?" she asked. "You've been sneezing all afternoon."

William dropped his hand and turned his head to look at her.

"I'm all right," he said.

"You sound rather congested. I really think you caught a cold when you were soaked through this morning."

"No, I don't get colds. It would take more than a little rain to— Achoo!"

"Bless you," Alice said, appearing suddenly. "Well, the bazaar was a huge success, and I'm expressing my sincerest gratitude to both of you for volunteering your time and merchandise."

"It was fun," Bailey said. "I especially enjoyed meeting Mary Margaret."

William mumbled something inaudible under his breath. Neither Bailey nor Alice asked him what he'd said.

"William," Alice said, "give me Mary Margaret's hat and I'll take it to her. She's over at a booth selling unusual hair clips. They're trying to pack up, but she can't decide whether she wants a barrette with a plastic giraffe or a turtle in a top hat."

William retrieved the hat from beneath the table and gave it to his sister. The delivery was accompanied by a loud "Achoo!"

"You *did* catch a cold," Alice said.

"Don't be silly," Bailey said, waving one hand breezily in the air. "William has informed me that cold germs wouldn't dare invade his macho body."

"Oh, do tell," Alice said.

William glared at each of them in turn.

"I'm hungry," Alice said. "Why don't we go out and get something to eat? Yes, that's an excellent idea."

"Oh, well, I don't think—" Bailey began.

"No, I—" William said at the same time.

"I'll call Raymond," Alice went on, as though neither of them had spoken, "and see if he's free to join us. It'll be fun."

"Don't you have to supervise the cleanup?" William said.

"No, I have volunteers for that. I'll give Mary Margaret her hat, find a phone, and be back in a flash." She hurried away.

"But—" Bailey said, pointing one finger in the air. Then she shrugged. "Well, a person does have to eat, I suppose."

"Don't get so excited," William said dryly. "You *are* going to be in the company of some very nice people, you know."

"Oh, I realize that," she said quickly. "It's just that it's been a long, tiring day. The noise level alone in this place was enough to cause exhaustion. I'm going to eat and run—right home to a bath and a quiet evening. My reluctance to go have dinner wasn't personal."

Yes, it was, she thought in the next instant. Alice's suggestion that they all go out hadn't conjured up mental images of delicious hot food. No, it had represented only the fact that she was going to spend further hours in close proximity to William Lansing.

And *that* was not a good idea.

William had an extremely unsettling effect on her. She knew it, didn't like it, and was thoroughly peeved at herself because of it. She was asking for trouble by agreeing to go out to dinner.

Well, maybe not. Alice and Raymond would be there, and the old saying that there was safety in numbers should hold true.

William sat down on his folding chair again and waited for the sneeze he could feel threatening to erupt.

He felt lousy, he thought. He had most definitely caught a cold from being soaked to the skin that morning. He hadn't had a cold for many years, and he was not about to acknowledge aloud the existence of this one.

It was embarrassing, to say the least. Bailey had been trapped in the same rainstorm, and *she* wasn't sneezing her head off. He would come across as a wimp if he admitted that he was indeed paying the price for getting wet and chilled. No way. He'd go out to dinner and be his usual cheerful, charming self.

And that was another thing, he mused, frowning. Bailey had scrambled to cover her tracks, had produced excuses as to why she wasn't thrilled to be joining the group for a meal. But the fact remained that her first reaction had been a negative one.

It wasn't a personal rejection, she'd said. Well, he was taking it as one. His head was pounding, his throat was scratchy, and he was in no mood to attempt to find a place to put the knowledge that Bailey would rather go home alone than go out to dinner with him.

Stop it, he told himself. He'd already decided that it would not be wise to see Bailey again. So what differ-

ence did it make whether or not she wanted to go to
dinner? None. But, damn it, *why* didn't she want to go
to dinner with him?

Just then, Alice reappeared. "All set. I forgot to ask
you two if you had a preference for a particular kind of
food, so I picked a family place that serves a bit of
everything." She rattled off the name of the restaurant
and instructions for finding it. "Let's go. I'm really
starving. Goodness, we'll look like a caravan. We'll have
four vehicles for four people. Do you want to double
up?"

"No," Bailey and William said in unison.

"Oh, well, whatever. We'll meet inside the restaurant. The first one there should get a table. Okay?
Come on, let's do it. We, my sweets, are out of here."

Twenty minutes later, the trio was seated at a table in
a pleasant restaurant that had a country decor.

The tables were covered in country-blue tablecloths,
with small, old-fashioned oil lamps in the center of
each. The walls boasted wooden animals, pictures of
farms and fields, and several brightly colored quilts.
Waitresses in long blue gingham dresses and perky white
dust caps scurried back and forth.

"So, where's Raymond?" William asked Alice.

"He'll be here. The traffic is bad, you know."

"Have you met Raymond, Bailey?" William said.

"Yes. He picked Alice up at aerobics once, when her
car was being serviced. He's very nice. If I ever need an
attorney, I'll know who to call."

"Raymond is a brilliant attorney," Alice said, smiling. "Not only that, but he's good-looking as all get-out. The phrase *tall, dark and handsome* was invented to apply to him."

"Brother," William said, shaking his head.

"I'm delighted," Alice said, wiggling her eyebrows, "that Raymond Wilson is *not* my brother. Oh, there he is." She waved one hand in the air.

Raymond strode to the table and greeted Bailey and William, but didn't sit down.

"Alice," he said, "something came up. I received an overseas phone call before I left the house, and I need to get a file from my office so I can iron out some kinks for one of my clients and call them back. I really don't have time to eat."

Alice jumped to her feet, nearly toppling over her chair in the process.

"My, my," she said, "isn't that a shame? I'll go with you, Raymond. I wouldn't feel right sitting here enjoying my meal while you're slaving away. We'll eat later." She grabbed his arm. "We'd better hurry. Goodbye, Bailey. Goodbye, William. Thanks again for taking part in the bazaar."

"But—" Bailey began. She didn't get to finish her sentence. Alice was already hustling away with Raymond in tow.

A waitress appeared at the table.

"Your party of four is getting smaller by the minute," she said. "Would you like something to drink while you're waiting for the others?"

"The four are now officially two," William said. "If you'll bring a couple of menus, we'll order."

"You've got it," the waitress said, then walked away.

Darn, the situation had gotten entirely out of hand, Bailey thought. Her safety-in-numbers shield was coming undone. She did *not* want to be here alone with William.

Yes, she did, she finally admitted to herself. She wanted to be here alone with William Lansing very, very much.

And the realization of that fact was frightening.

Outside, Alice and Raymond stopped before separating to go to their own vehicles.

"How'd I do?" Raymond said.

"It was an Academy Award performance."

"One of these days," he said, chuckling, "I might learn how to say no to you, Alice. I don't like meddlesome matchmaking, and here I am giving it my all."

"You were fantastic. Let's go somewhere sinfully expensive and have dinner."

"Your treat. We actors get paid a bundle. Alice, this is really crazy. Bailey Crandell is a career-oriented woman. You know how firm William's stand is on finding his old-fashioned girl. That is not a matched set we left in there. Not even close."

"You never know, my darling husband. You just never know."

Three

Bailey buried her nose in the tall, narrow menu the waitress had left, reading all the fine print describing each and every choice available.

When the waitress reappeared, Bailey ordered fried shrimp and a baked potato. William said he'd have the same. The woman left, then quickly returned with tossed salads.

Bailey busied herself with the crisp vegetables. She took a bite, rearranged the rest, then repeated the performance.

William watched her. He got the impression that her preoccupation with the salad was her way of virtually ignoring him.

Well, forget that, he thought. Yes, he'd decided that the best plan of action regarding Bailey was to not see her again after today.

But, because of circumstances beyond his control, he was now alone with her, having dinner. This was, in essence, one of those casual dates he'd decided against.

He hadn't set up the evening this way, but there they were, and he'd be damned if he'd be ignored.

A teenage boy came to the table, mumbled, "Excuse me," and lit the small oil lamp. A golden glow now emanated from it.

Oh, dear, Bailey thought, whoever said that soft light was flattering to women hadn't bothered to take notice of the effect it had on men. Well, some men. More precisely, William Lansing.

The shadows cast by the flickering flame made his tanned, rugged features appear as though they were chiseled from stone.

Those mesmerizing gray eyes were warm, bottomless pools tempting her to simply surrender and succumb to their beckoning depths.

His thick, dark hair was now a shade so rich that there would probably be no place for it on an artist's spectrum of color.

William Lansing, she mused, was magnificent. Oh, how she wanted to reach across the small table and trace each of his features with her fingertips, etching them indelibly on her mind.

She wanted to feel his lips on hers, to feel his strong arms enfolding her, crushing her softness to the hard contours of his body. She was being consumed by a flame of desire as hot and intense as the one in the lamp on that table.

No! her mind hammered. Her fantasies were taking her down a dangerous path. She could not, would not, change the course of her life, the direction she was going in, the goals she fully intended to achieve.

She must, she *would,* resist the lure, the masculine magnetism, of William Lansing.

"So," William said, jarring her from her thoughts, "fill me in on how Sweet Fantasy came into existence."

"It's not a particularly interesting story. Do you really want to know?"

"I really *do* want to know, Bailey," he said quietly, looking directly into her eyes.

With every bit of willpower she could muster, Bailey tore her gaze from his and directed her attention to the oil lamp. "I graduated from UCLA," she said, "with a degree in business management, having decided that I wanted to someday have my own business. I did not, however, have a handle on what it should be. So, I job-hopped for about a year."

"Research."

"Exactly. The pay was minimum wage, I was usually a cashier or stock person, but the experience was invaluable. Admittedly, I got discouraged at times, because I was creating an ever-growing list of things that I did *not* wish to focus on. My parents were wonderful during that year, very supportive. My father died a year ago, but he was there to see Sweet Fantasy become a reality.''

Bailey stopped speaking when the waitress appeared with their dinners, and for the next several minutes they ate in silence, nodding in approval at the taste of the hot, delicious food.

"Go on with your story," William finally said.

"In actuality, Sweet Fantasy was a gathering of ideas from a half-dozen different jobs. In a craft shop, I learned the multitude of uses for baskets, cans, tins with lids, knew who manufactured the best quality for the most reasonable price.

"In a gift shop came a thorough understanding of the commercial influence surrounding holidays. Plus, I observed daily buying habits of harried and hassled working mothers, weekend fathers, teenagers, and senior citizens on fixed incomes.

"A two-month stint as a gofer in an advertising agency afforded me endless information on the psychology of advertising, why some approaches work and others don't."

"I'm very impressed," William said, nodding. "Then?"

After pausing to take a bite, Bailey continued her tale. She'd had, she told William, a small inheritance from her grandmother and that had enabled her to launch Sweet Fantasy.

She'd met with a multitude of unexpected red tape at every turn: zoning, regulations regarding the selling of food, the procedures for gaining permission to put her logo sticker on everything she sold, including trademarked items from registered firms.

Some of the candy and other sweets she sold were made locally, others were flown in from across the country, produced by those she considered to be the very best in the field.

She'd tackled each step in turn, finally arriving at the day Sweet Fantasy could officially open for business.

"At last my Pegasus flew, and that, sir, is my story," she said, smiling. "Sweet Fantasy is three years old. Every penny I've made has gone back into it to expand the selection of candies and other goodies. I have a matchbox-size apartment and a limited wardrobe, but I don't mind, because I'm concentrating on my goal, my dream."

William leaned back in his chair as the waitress removed the plates. They ordered apple pie and coffee, which was quickly delivered.

He was truly impressed with what Bailey had done, William mused, taking a bite of pie. Her blue eyes had virtually sparkled as she related her story of how her business had been born.

But while a portion of him admired and respected her for all she had accomplished, another section of his being was feeling more dismal by the moment. The Pegasus dancing and flying in his mental vision was growing bigger and stronger.

Any lingering hope he might have been unconsciously clinging to that Bailey was not as totally committed to her career as he had thought was now gone. A relationship with her was a lost cause, and there was no point in attempting to give one room to grow. He was going to walk away from Bailey and forget her...if possible.

"All right, William," Bailey said pleasantly, "now it's your turn. What made you decide to become an investment broker?"

He shrugged. "It's in my genes, I guess. My father started his own company on a shoestring, then slowly proved his worth, established a reputation for excellence with hard work, intelligence and sound reasoning."

Bailey nodded.

"When I was eight years old," William continued, "my dad bought me some stock and said it was mine to do with as I wished. I was hooked right there on the spot. I sold my stock at double what my dad had bought it for, then reinvested in other stocks, beginning to build a diversified high-risk-low-risk portfolio. There was never any doubt in my mind that I'd join my father's firm some day."

William cleared his throat before continuing. "When I was ten, my father died of a heart attack. He'd been warned by his doctors that he should slow down, but he ignored the advice, just kept on at full speed. He'd expanded to having overseas clients, and he was gone more than he was home. I think he had a perpetual case of jet lag.

"During the last year of his life, I can't remember him saying anything to me other than, 'What day is this?' He eventually paid the price for what had become an obsession with success."

"I see," Bailey said quietly. "And your mother?"

A shadow of something that Bailey couldn't quite put a name to flickered across William's face and in his expressive gray eyes, then was gone. It had happened so quickly, she wondered if she'd imagined it, if it had been nothing more than a play of the light from the oil lamp.

"My mother," William went on, "worked side by side with my father from the beginning of Lansing Investments. She continually told Alice and me that as soon as the company was firmly established, they'd hire someone to take her place and she'd stay home to care for her family.

"That time came and went, as my mother was caught up in the challenge and excitement, just as my father was. She stepped in when he died and took over the company. She wasn't home much, because her main interest was the overseas division. She lives in London now, and the foreign clients are managed by her."

"Who took care of you and Alice?"

"A long string of housekeepers who came and went. Alice worked at Lansing Investments until she married Raymond. Since then she's tended to their two kids, their home, done a lot of volunteer projects, that sort of thing. Alice's children will have fond memories of coming home after school and being able to share their day with their mother."

William paused for a moment, then went on. "Alice is a rare individual. They don't seem to make wives and mothers like her anymore. Not very often, anyway.'' He looked intently at Bailey, studying her face for a reaction to what he had said.

''No, they don't,'' she said, without a hint of a smile. ''That your sister is fulfilled in the role she chose is wonderful. Many women...'' She hesitated, then shifted her gaze to her napkin, which lay on the table. She began to pleat it with the fingers of one hand, then smoothed it in the next instant. When she spoke again, her voice was hushed to the point that William had to lean forward to hear her. Her eyes were still riveted on the napkin, as though she had never seen one before.

''Many woman,'' she finally continued, ''smother their dreams, until their fantasies of what they could be, might achieve in the outside world, die from lack of attention, or acknowledgment that they ever existed.''

She slowly raised her eyes to meet William's.

''Do you know what happens to those women when the last or only child leaves home, William? When they're faced with the empty nest? And then—even worse—if the man, their husband, either dies or leaves her for another way of life or another woman? They're lost souls, those dedicated mothers and homemakers. They have no purpose, no direction. They have nothing...nothing.''

Say something, Lansing, he mentally hollered at himself. Counterattack. Present the opposite side of the coin to Bailey's incredibly negative viewpoint. *But, damn it, he didn't know what to say.*

He'd been caught totally off guard by the intensity of Bailey's feelings on the subject. This was a strange puzzle, and there were definitely pieces missing.

"Bailey..." he began.

"Goodness," she said, forcing a smile that barely materialized. "I certainly got on my soapbox, didn't I? Just forget all that. I—"

"Achoo!"

"There you go again. William, you should be home in bed, starting on juice and aspirin, and I'm exhausted from the long day at the bazaar. Let's just call it a night, shall we?"

She picked up her purse and slid her chair back, leaving William no choice but to signal to the waitress for the check.

Outside in the parking lot, Bailey thanked William for the dinner, said it had been a pleasure to meet him and share his company, then spun around and hurried toward her car.

William watched her go, a deep frown on his face.

Monday, after a dreary, cloudy Sunday, was clear and sunny. The forecast called for more rain, but by noon there were no dark clouds in the bright blue sky.

Business at Lansing Investments was brisk, keeping the staff of William, three other brokers, and their secretaries, hopping. William's hop, however, was definitely running out of steam.

"Achoo!"

William's secretary, Betty Hunt, was a plump woman in her fifties. She had four grandchildren who were, she was continually announcing to everyone who would stand still long enough to listen, the brightest, most beautiful children ever born.

Betty stood in front of William's large, gleaming mahogany desk. She frowned, shook her head, then made a *tsk*ing sound she'd perfected over many years. It spoke volumes.

"You're a contagious germ, William Lansing," she said. "The plaster is going to crack from your sneezing. Due to the fact that you're a typical single man, you don't take proper care of yourself."

"I certainly do," he said indignantly, glaring up at her. "I spent all day yesterday doctoring this damn cold. All I managed to do was practice my sneezing until it was Olympic caliber."

"Well, it sounds to me like you should have stayed in bed today, too. You're obviously in lousy shape, to have been cut off at the knees by the common cold. It's sad, very sad."

"Spare me the sermon," William said. "Save it to use at my funeral, because I'll be dead by midnight. I can feel it in my aching bones."

"You'll have to postpone dying. I need your signature on these letters."

"You're heartless, Betty. You're going to flunk grandmotherdom. Could I have a little sympathy? It's hard to breathe, you know, when you have a cold, and

I have something of extreme importance to do tonight."

"Big date?"

"Well, no, not exactly. I'm just planning to drop by and see someone."

"Oh? Who?"

"Bailey Crandell. She owns Sweet Fantasy."

"Really? My grandchildren love to go to Sweet Fantasy. So do I, as a matter of fact." She paused and shook her head. "Bailey Crandell. It's doesn't work, William. She's not old-fashioned, and everyone knows your stand on old-fashioned. Bailey Crandell owns and operates an up-and-coming business. How can seeing her be so important?"

"It's complicated, Betty, and I don't have the energy to explain it to you. Hell, I can't even figure out how to explain it to myself."

"Well, I certainly can't picture you with Bailey Crandell."

"Achoo!" was William's final contribution to the conversation.

Bailey smiled as she watched the vibrant rainbows dance across the interior of the store. The late-afternoon sunlight poured through the sparkling windows, where multicolored stained-glass sun-catchers in varying designs hung, ready and waiting to produce the rainbows.

She'd been busy with customers from the moment she unlocked the front door that morning, and hadn't had an opportunity to perform her daily ritual with her bright blue feather duster.

Mondays were typically slow, giving evidence to the validity of the market research Bailey had studied. People had a tendency to overeat on the weekend, then make Monday-morning resolutions to behave themselves. On Tuesday they wavered, and by Wednesday business at Sweet Fantasy was brisk.

Bailey worked alone on Mondays, because extra help usually just wasn't necessary. But today had been different, with heavy traffic. It was the rainy weather on the weekend, she surmised. People had been housebound, they'd probably had to cancel plans for outings, and now they were facing another long workweek. They deserved a treat to perk up their moods, so they headed for Sweet Fantasy.

She'd welcomed the hectic pace of the day, as it hadn't allowed her to think of anything beyond meeting the needs of the customers.

The day before had seemed endless, as she'd cleaned her apartment, washed clothes and thought about William Lansing. No matter how hard she'd tried to shove him from her mental vision, he'd refused to budge.

By the time she'd crawled wearily into bed, she'd been none too happy with William for invading her usually peaceful Sunday. His pushy presence was all his fault, she'd somehow convinced herself, and she'd awakened that morning out of sorts and totally annoyed with Mr. Lansing.

He'd even followed her into the shower, she silently fumed, whipping the feather duster over the shelves. There she'd stood, naked as the day she was born, warm water pouring over her, and seeing William with crystal clarity in her mind's eye.

With a cluck of disgust, she continued her chore, flicking her trusty duster over jars of sour balls, licorice whips, taffy, honey-coated peanuts and other scrumptious delicacies.

The tin boxes and wicker baskets were next, and then the long, glass-fronted display case.

The aroma of coffee wafted through the air, and she inhaled the rich scent, speeding up the duster's journey over the counter and the cash register.

Holding a mug of eagerly anticipated cinnamon coffee in a pale blue ceramic mug with white clouds and a flying Pegasus on it, she settled into the white wicker rocking chair behind the counter.

She'd taken only one delicious sip when the tinkling bell over the door sounded, announcing that someone had entered the store.

With a resigned sigh, she set the mug on the small table next to the rocker and got to her feet.

Her heart began to beat a rapid tattoo, and she blinked once, wondering if she was only imagining that William Lansing was standing in the middle of the shop.

"Hello, Bailey," he said.

Oh, good night, he *was* real, she thought, and so was the warm fluttering deep within her. What that man could do to her simply by *being* was sinful. In faded jeans and a pale green knit shirt that accentuated his tan and his thick, dark hair, he was magnificent.

Darn it, she didn't want him to be there. She had been attempting, to no avail, to forget she'd ever met him, to erase from her memory his ability to unsettle her, cause a heated flush of desire to stain her cheeks, pin her in place with those incredible gray eyes.

Go away, William Lansing, she mentally ordered.

"This is quite a place," he said, snapping Bailey back to attention. He continued his scrutiny of the store, his gaze lingering on a wall that had an enchanting mural of blue sky, white clouds and a large Pegasus flying through the heavens. "Very, very nice."

He was stalling for time, William admitted to himself. At the moment Bailey appeared behind the counter, he'd felt as though he'd run full-force into a brick wall. The air had seemed to swish from his lungs, and his heart had begun imitating a bongo drum.

He shouldn't be here, he knew, but it would take a gun pointed at his head to get him to leave. Damn, this was crazy.

Bailey was not the type of woman he was hoping to find. The strange sensual spell she was capable of weaving around him was dangerous, and if he had half a brain he wouldn't come within ten miles of her.

But here he was. *Brainless Lansing,* he thought dryly, *right smack-dab in the middle of Sweet Fantasy.* And there was Bailey, beautiful, fresh, all decked out in a ruffled bib apron over a pale blue blouse.

"Hello, William," Bailey said. "May I help you with something?"

No, he thought, because he had a sinking feeling in his gut that he was rapidly approaching the point of being beyond help. He'd been pulled to Bailey by invisible threads, unable to stay away.

But *she* certainly wasn't going to know the effect she had on him. No way. All he had to do now was produce a reasonably reasonable reason for having shown up there.

"Yes," he said, starting toward her. "Yes, you certainly can help me. I'm here to—" He stopped at the counter and looked directly into her eyes.

He was here to pull her into his arms, he thought hazily, and kiss her. He was there to nestle her close, feel her soft, feminine curves fitting perfectly against him. He was there to appease the ache low in his body—by making love with her.

He was here, he thought, forcing himself back to reality, to be labeled certifiably insane, then shipped off to the farm.

Bailey cocked her head and confusion was evident on her face as the seconds ticked by and William still didn't answer.

"William?"

"Achoo!"

Bailey jerked in surprise. "Goodness! Bless you!"

Before William could answer, the bell over the door tinkled, and a man entered the shop. William stepped away from the counter to allow the customer to approach the display case.

William narrowed his eyes as his gaze swept over the man.

Phoenix yuppie, he thought sullenly. *Suave, smooth, custom-tailored suit, phony as a three-dollar bill. Graying at the temples. Hell, nobody turned gray that perfectly, except maybe Cary Grant. This guy probably painted the gray on there.*

William wandered around the store, looking at but not really seeing, the individual items. He had one eye and both ears cocked in the direction of the counter.

"There you are," Bailey said, handing the man a sack and change. "I hope you enjoy your Turtles." She smiled.

For Pete's sake, William thought, she wasn't auditioning for a toothpaste commercial. A pleasant, professional, *small* smile would have done the job.

"I always enjoy your splendid delicacies, Bailey," the man said.

Bailey! Bailey? William thought. Mr. Painted Gray Temples was really pushing it. William shook his head and stared through the glass case at a long, narrow tray of chocolate suckers in the shapes of animals.

He was crazy, totally nuts, he admitted to himself. He'd met Bailey Crandell only a couple of days ago, and now he was acting like a jealous lover. He was mentally behaving like a jerk, and enough was enough.

"Goodbye," Bailey was saying. "Thank you. I hope it doesn't start raining again."

"See you soon," the man said cheerfully, then turned and left the store.

William crossed the floor to stand opposite Bailey again.

"Well, back to the purpose of your visit," Bailey said. "Why are you here?"

He'd come to sweep her off her feet, Bailey thought dreamily, to plant a searing kiss on her rosebud lips, then carry her in his strong arms toward the sunset. Oh, for heaven's sake, how ridiculous, she told herself.

"I came," William said, "to buy some hard candy. That's just what I need to wipe out the last of the sore throat I have from this cold. It's not a big-time cold, you understand. I feel perfectly fine, but it's annoying to be sneezing so often, and my throat is scratchy."

"Hard candy," Bailey repeated, nodding slowly.

It was *not* disappointment she was registering, she told herself. So what if William was more interested in her hard candy than he was in her? That was just fine. No problem.

But why did she feel as though another dark cloud had suddenly formed directly above her?

She should be relieved that William obviously didn't intend to pursue the issue of the attraction between them. She'd sell him some candy and send him on his way, and that would be that.

"Hard candy, it is," she said, striving for a breezy, cheerful tone of voice. "If you'll step down to the far wall, you can pick your flavor."

They moved at the same time to meet by the shelves. The counter was no longer between them, and they were both acutely aware of that fact.

"There you are," Bailey said, with a sweep of her arm. "You can see what we have to offer."

William bent over slightly and peered at the multitude of jars.

Bailey savored the scent of his woodsy after-shave, combined with an aroma of fresh air and soap. He was so close she could see the shadow of his end-of-the-day beard, and the individual strands of his thick black hair.

Heat thrummed low within her, then swept upward, causing her breasts to feel heavy, achy, in need of a soothing touch.

She should step back, she knew, put more distance between herself and William, erect a mental barrier as solid as the counter had been. That was what she *should* do, but she wasn't going to budge.

William straightened and turned to look at Bailey, meeting her gaze.

"You have a great selection of hard candy," he said. "I want... What I want is..." His voice trailed off. "Ah, hell..."

He framed her face in his hands, then slowly, slowly, lowered his head toward hers. Bailey shivered in anticipation of the moment when William's lips would at last, *at last,* claim hers. Her lashes drifted down, her lips were slightly parted, and her heart was beating in a wild cadence.

Yes, yes, yes, her mind hummed.

"No," William said, causing Bailey's eyes to fly open.

To her shock and dismay, William abruptly released her and stepped backward. She swayed unsteadily for a moment, then frowned.

No? she mentally repeated. No, he'd decided he didn't want to kiss her?

"Bailey, it wouldn't be fair to kiss you when I'm a walking germ. I'd feel terrible if you caught my cold." He took a jar of peppermint balls from the shelf. "I'll buy these, then take my nasty rotten germs home." He paused. "I want to kiss you. I hope you know that. Lord, do I ever want to kiss you."

"Oh," she said, smiling warmly. "Well, the feeling is mutual."

He matched her smile, and they continued to look directly into each other's eyes for another long moment. Then they walked to their original spots—Bailey behind the counter, William in front. But the counter no longer seemed like a barrier. It might as well have been invisible. They felt connected, once again caught in a mysterious, sensuous web woven of threads they couldn't see.

The transaction completed, William picked up the sack, then suddenly chuckled, a grin breaking across his face. Bailey looked at him questioningly.

"My head is so congested," he said, "I can hardly breathe. Man, oh, man, would you have been in a tight spot trying to explain my dead body to the cops." He burst out laughing.

"Oh, my goodness!" Bailey said, unable to contain her own merriment. "The mental scenario you're painting is hysterical. 'I killed him with a kiss, Officer. Hey, if you've got it, you've got it, ya know what I mean?' Oh, dear!"

Their mingled laughter danced through the air.

"Well," he said finally. "I'll be seeing you."

She nodded.

"So long."

She nodded again. William still didn't move.

"Bailey, would you go out to dinner with me Saturday night? I swear there won't be a cold germ left in my body by then. Seven o'clock?"

"Yes," she said, her voice little more than a whisper. "I'm in the book, apartment 410. Yes, seven o'clock."

They looked at each other for another long, heart-stopping moment.

William finally spun around and crossed the store. The bells tinkled above the door as he opened it, and then he was gone.

The sudden silence was oppressive.

It was so quiet now, Bailey thought, so still, as though Sweet Fantasy had been lifted up and away, flung into space, where no one else existed but her.

"Oh, for crying out loud, Bailey," she scolded herself. "You're not Dorothy, and you don't have a dog named Toto. This isn't Kansas, it's Phoenix, Arizona."

She was, she knew, physically and emotionally shaken. She felt as though the very foundation on which she'd built her existence had been weakened by the force of William's emergence into her life.

That foundation had been solid and strong, consciously constructed by decisions made and a path chosen. Her focus, her energies, were directed toward the continued success and growth of Sweet Fantasy, and there was no room for a serious relationship, a husband and children.

She'd been doing fine...until William. She'd been fulfilled, she'd had all she needed to be content ... until William. The idea that she might be lonely in her aloneness had not even been entertained ... until William.

Dear heaven, what was happening to her?

Even more important, what was she going to do?

If she refused to see William again, if she ran as fast and as far from him as possible, she'd be admitting to herself that the foundation was indeed beginning to crumble.

No! It wasn't!

She knew who she was, where she was headed, what she wanted.

To have been thrown off kilter by a dynamic man who made her acutely aware of her own femininity was only human. But to be so frightened, feeling so threatened, was absurd.

Bailey lifted her chin and squared her shoulders.

I am woman, she thought, nodding decisively. She could see William, be with William, even be kissed and held by William, and not lose touch with her true inner self.

Everything was once more under control.

William drove toward his apartment, his thoughts centered on Bailey Crandell.

He was not, he realized, coming to any grand conclusions or great revelations about Bailey. He was simply thinking of her.

He could see, as clearly as if she was sitting in front of him, her lovely smile, her soft, short dark curls, and those blue eyes that turned him inside out. He could hear her delightful laughter.

Oh, yes, he mused, the heat was there again, coiling low in his body as he envisioned taking Bailey into his arms and finally kissing her delectable, beckoning lips. But he'd want more. He'd want to make love with her.

No doubt about it, he thought, nodding—Bailey Crandell had had a tremendous impact on him, far more intense than anything he'd ever experienced. He should be concerned about that, because Bailey was the wrong woman for him. But—ah, hell, he'd worry about that part later.

He switched on the radio, pressed a button to select a country station and instantly began to sing at full volume—albeit terribly off key—in a duet with Garth Brooks about beer and the blues.

But as he tapped his fingertips on the steering wheel in time to the music, he thought about the fact that he didn't have any blues. No sir, he was a happy man. Not overly bright regarding the subject of Bailey, he supposed, but happy.

And right smack-dab in the middle of his mental circle of sunshine was the image of Bailey Crandell.

Four

Bailey had not slept well, and she arrived at Sweet Fantasy the next morning with a throbbing headache. Her mother, Deborah Crandell, was behind the counter, signing a receipt for the daily delivery of dark and light chocolate, vanilla and maple fudge.

The rich aroma of cinnamon coffee greeted Bailey, but this morning it did not produce the usual smile.

"Good morning, Mother," she said. She moved aside to allow the delivery man to pass, absently telling him to have a nice day. "Are we all set to open up?"

Deborah turned to smile at her daughter.

Deborah Crandell was five feet two inches tall and had the delicate features and slender figure her daughter had inherited.

Her once-blond hair was now silver and worn in becoming soft waves that capped her head. Her eyes were blue and, like Bailey's, sparkled when she smiled.

She was wearing an outfit that matched Bailey's—a ruffled apron over a pale blue blouse and white slacks.

"Hello, darling," she said. "Did you see the dozens of material squares on the table in the back room? I finished sewing the hems. I think material liners will be a lovely addition to the baskets. Very classy."

"Yes, I saw them, and I appreciate the many hours you spent on them."

"Which I thoroughly enjoyed, as you well know." Deborah paused, frowning. "Honey, is there something wrong? You're rather pale, and it seems like you're not your usual peppy self."

"I'm fine," Bailey said. "I just have a headache this morning. I'm sure it will pass soon."

"I brought in some fresh doughnuts to go with the coffee. I know you, Miss Crandell. You haven't had a bite of breakfast. Some food will help your head and perk you right up."

"No, I'm really not hungry."

"That's no excuse, dear. Eat. I'll open up the store and take care of things out here. Get some coffee and a doughnut, then go in the back room and relax. You can start your day all over again."

It was easier to eat, Bailey decided, than argue.

"All right, Mother," she said, smiling. "I'll do as I'm told." She started toward the back room. "Call me if you need me."

"Shoo," her mother said.

The rear area of the store had been designed by Bailey to provide a maximum of storage space and still allow room for a small refrigerator, a microwave oven and a table and chairs.

To make every inch possible available for jars, tins and bags on the wooden shelves that lined the walls, a multitude of baskets were hung from the ceiling on bamboo chains with plastic hooks on the ends.

With a weary sigh, Bailey sank onto one of the chairs at the table, then took a sip of the steaming coffee. In the next instant her head snapped up at the distant sound of the bells on the front door tinkling. She relaxed again, knowing her mother would tend to the customer.

Deborah had blossomed at Sweet Fantasy. Her mother had been a lost soul after the death of her husband the year before. She had seemed to wither, to grow old before Bailey's very eyes.

But now? A loving smile touched Bailey's lips. Now her mother glowed, was full of energy and purpose and was enthusiastically involved in the nurturing of Bailey's business. Deborah felt fulfilled and needed again, and the aura of happiness surrounding her was genuine.

Bailey took a bite of a buttermilk doughnut, then stared into space.

How strange, she thought, that a nonhuman entity such as a business, housed in a building, could give so much to the people connected to it. Millie, a widowed friend of her mother's, the two college girls who worked part-time, and herself—all had sought and found exactly what they needed at Sweet Fantasy.

And Bailey herself was as happy as a bee in clover. Right? Her years of hard work and meticulous research were paying off, and there was nothing missing from the picture of her existence in her mind's eye. Right?

She took another bite of her doughnut.

Still, she'd like to know why she was suddenly looking for the reassurance that positive answers to those questions would bring her. She couldn't remember ever questioning the structure of her life before. She'd gotten all of this under control the previous day. But she still felt so different, so off kilter.

She narrowed her eyes and pursed her lips.

She'd felt that way ever since meeting William Lansing.

Cancel the Saturday-night date, a little inner voice whispered. Refuse to see the man again.

But she wanted William to walk in the door that very moment, a stronger inner voice answered, and she wanted to be with him on Saturday night.

Remember that Sweet Fantasy required all your mental and physical energies, the little voice countered.

But was Sweet Fantasy really enough? the stronger voice taunted.

Bailey drained her mug, then marched to the front of the store, determined to ignore the muddled mess in her mind.

The day seemed endless. Bailey's headache improved, but her mood did not. Her smile was forced. It felt as though it had been painted on her face.

Deborah left an hour before closing to keep a dental appointment, and Bailey busied herself waiting on customers and restocking shelves. She glanced often at her watch, willing the minutes to tick away and announce the end of the workday.

William walked along the sidewalk leading to Sweet Fantasy, his long legs covering the distance in short order. He glared at the empty parking places he passed, none of which had been available when he was forced to park three blocks away.

He was not, he knew, in a chipper frame of mind. While he'd have liked to blame his dark mood on his cold, he couldn't, as the last dregs of it had disappeared completely during the day.

No, it wasn't the common cold that was causing his grumpy disposition, it was Bailey. Bailey, Bailey, Bailey. A pesky woman, that was what she was. She was constantly hovering in his mental vision.

There was that smile, that sunshine-on-a-rainy-day smile. He could hear her lovely laughter, could actually smell the aroma of her light floral cologne.

And her lips? Damn, those lips and the remembrance of the near-kiss they'd almost shared, were so vivid that the heated desire churning low in his body was driving him crazy, refusing to be extinguished.

Go away, Miss Sweet Fantasy, he ordered.

Brilliant, Lansing, he thought in the next instant. Why was he now only half a block away from the woman in question, with every intention of entering Sweet Fantasy as quickly as possible? Because he was a lunatic, that was why. It was sad but true.

He'd left the office early, despite the stack of files and telephone messages needing his attention, to work on his current project at his house, then settle in to enjoy a televised baseball game.

Twenty minutes after changing into jeans and a knit shirt, he'd thrown up his hands in defeat, realizing that a pleasant evening alone at home was out of the question, due to the mental menace known as Bailey Crandell.

Can't beat 'em? he thought, stopping in front of Sweet Fantasy. *Join 'em.* Maybe if he spent a little time with Bailey now, he could hightail it home in a bit, see at least a few innings of the ball game and regain his usually pleasant disposition.

He opened the door and entered the store, his jaw set in a tight, determined line.

Bailey picked up the keys that would, at last, lock up Sweet Fantasy for the night. As she started to move from behind the counter, the door opened and William appeared.

They acknowledged each other with matching frowns.

"I was just about to close," Bailey said with a slight edge in her voice.

"Go for it," William said, sweeping one arm through the air. His frown remained firmly in place.

Bailey tended to the door, flipped the sign over to Closed, then turned to face William, not a hint of a smile on her face.

A long, strained, oppressively silent minute passed.

Then, slowly, very slowly, a smile began to tug at William's lips, finally spreading into a grin.

"I do believe," he said, "that Miss Manners would say it is less than socially acceptable behavior to go a-callin' when one is in a crummy mood."

Bailey smiled. "She would also say, I imagine, that one should receive guests graciously, putting aside one's personally lousy frame of mind." She paused. "Hello, William Lansing."

"Hello, Bailey Crandell. Do you want to talk about why you're a grouch?"

"No. Do you?"

"No." He closed the distance between them and framed her face in his hands. His smile faded, and his voice was low and rumbly when he spoke again. "No, I don't want to talk about anything right now, except to tell you that the last trace of my cold has gone, taking the germs with it. We have unfinished business, Bailey, that doesn't call for discussion."

"Oh" was all Bailey managed to say, with a little puff of air.

Then William dipped his head . . . and kissed her.

A shimmer of warmth coursed through Bailey the instant William's lips touched hers. Her lashes drifted

down at the same moment her arms floated up to en-
circle his neck. He dropped his hands from her face,
wrapped his arms around her, then nestled her to him.
He parted her lips, their tongues met and passions flared
with intense heat.

Oh, William, Bailey's mind hummed. She'd waited
an eternity for this kiss, and it was beyond her wildest
dreams. The taste, the feel and the aroma of him,
crowded her senses, filled them to overflowing.

The kiss was searing, stealing the breath from her
body and logical reason from her mind. She'd been
transported to a sensual place, and it was ecstasy.

Bailey, William's mind thundered in time with his
pounding heart. This kiss was all he had known it would
be, and somehow it was more. It wasn't just a kiss, it
was an explosion of sensations that were causing him to
ache with wanting her.

She was returning the ardor of his kiss in kind, giving as much as she was receiving. She was a woman of
passion, and he gloried in knowing that passion was
being directed at him, given freely as a precious gift for
him to cherish.

Bailey felt so delicate, so small, he mused hazily.
There, in the circle of his arms, she was vulnerable, at
the mercy of his strength, which could crush her with
little effort. But no harm would come to Bailey Crandell, because he would protect her, care for her, stand
between her and anything that might hurt her.

When he made love to her, he would be gentle, ca-
ress her as he would the finest, most fragile china. Their

joining, he knew, would be like none before, and the mere image of it in his mind's eye was bringing him to the edge of his control. *Lord, how he wanted her.*

He tore his mouth from Bailey's and drew a harsh breath. With visibly shaking hands, he grasped her shoulders and eased her away from his body, instantly missing her softness.

"Bailey," he said, his voice a hoarse whisper.

She slowly lifted her lashes, and a groan escaped from William's throat when he saw the smoky hue of her blue eyes, which spoke of a desire that matched his own. Her lips were moist and slightly parted, beckoning to him to drink of their sweetness once again. Mustering all the willpower he possessed, he dropped his hands to his sides and took a step backward.

"Would you—" He cleared his throat. "Would you like to go grab a hamburger, then go shopping with me?"

Bailey blinked, then took a wobbly breath. "Shopping?"

"Yes. I moved into a house a month ago. I designed it with the help of an architect friend of mine, then had it built. I'm putting the finishing touches on the inside now, and tonight I want to buy towels, washcloths, bathroom rugs, that sort of thing. How does that sound?"

Bailey smiled, willing her heart to return to a normal tempo.

"It sounds like fun," she said. "But I thought single men hired decorators to take care of details like that."

"Not *this* single man. Let's go."

They ate hamburgers and French fries, and milk-shakes so thick they had to use spoons in place of straws. While they ate, they debated the merits of a controversial new movie, and good-naturedly argued about the book currently at the top of the best-seller lists. They then headed for the linens section of a large, high-quality department store.

"My goodness," Bailey said, standing in front of the towel display. "It's a rainbow. Look at all those gorgeous colors." She laughed. "Take one of each."

"It's tempting, but we have to coordinate, you know. There are three bathrooms in the house, each with a different accent color." He leaned forward and narrowed his eyes. "Now, let's see here..."

An hour later, Bailey wiggled her toes in her shoes to determine if they were still functioning. She held a stack of towels and washcloths in her arms and was wondering wearily how many more times William was going to change his mind and replace them with others.

She would never have believed, she thought, that a man would take the selection of bath towels so seriously. It was an interesting and endearing discovery about William, a depth to him that she hadn't known was there. But, oh, dear, she was tired.

"I think that does it," William said slowly. He glanced at Bailey, then did a quick double take, a frown instantly knitting his brows. "Oh, Bailey, I'm sorry. I got so caught up in this project, I didn't notice how exhausted you must be. Look, I'll pay for this stuff, and then I've got the perfect remedy to pep you up.''

"Oh?" she said, as William lifted the stacks of towels from her arms.

"Yep. I'm going to buy you the biggest hot fudge sundae in the city of Phoenix, Miss Crandell."

"Mr. Lansing," she said, smiling, "you've got yourself a deal."

The ice cream parlor that William drove to was called The Ice Cream Parlor, which caused Bailey to smile in delight. It had an old-fashioned decor—glass-covered tables surrounded by white wrought-iron chairs with red-and-white-checked padded seats. Quiet music drifted through the air, and Bailey quickly realized it was songs from the fifties and sixties.

"What a wonderful place," she said, after settling onto her chair. "Oh, listen, they're playing 'Chapel of Love.' The song before this one was 'Sixteen Candles.'"

William placed their order, then folded his arms on the top of the table. "Do you like this music?"

Bailey nodded. "The songs of that era made sense. You could understand the words, you could dance close together, and romance was high on the list of priorities."

"You're sounding a tad old-fashioned there, my dear," William said.

Before Bailey could reply, the waitress appeared carrying a tray with two tall ice-cream sundaes.

"Now is that, or is that not," William said, "a state-of-the-art hot fudge sundae?"

"Dig in," the waitress said, placing glasses of ice water on the table, along with napkins and spoons. "Polish off every bite, folks. The dessert chef, as he likes to be called, is very sensitive, and he gets crushed to the core when one of his creations isn't finished down to the last lick of the spoon." She smiled, then hurried away.

"It's gigantic," Bailey said, staring at the dessert. "Ice cream, hot fudge, whipped cream, nut sprinkles and a cherry on top. I'll never be able to eat all this."

William reached for his glass of water and took a deep swallow.

Oh, my word, Bailey thought, her gaze riveted on him, how was it possible that a man's throat, his neck—his Adam's apple, for crying out loud—could be so...so blatantly sexy? His neck was tanned and strong, perfectly proportioned to the wide width of his shoulders and the broad expanse of his chest. And below that chest? Now there was an intriguing, toe-curling question.

She dragged her sensuous thoughts back to the matter at hand, and watched as William picked up his spoon and took a good-sized bite of ice cream.

"Mmm..." he said, closing his eyes for a second and smiling. "Heaven itself. Go for it, Bailey."

She lifted the whipped cream-coated cherry by the stem and held it up for inspection before starting to move it toward her mouth. Her lips slightly parted, her hand stilled in midair as her eyes collided with William's.

All traces of humor were gone from William's gray eyes, replaced by the smoky hue of desire, sudden and intense. Heat suffused Bailey, and her heart began to race as she felt herself held immobile by the raw, earthy desire evident on William's face. As her hand began to tremble, she brought the cherry nearer her mouth, then closed her lips over its sweetness, pulling the stem free. She chewed and swallowed, her gaze riveted on William's.

"You left some whipped cream," he said, his voice very low and gritty.

He picked up a napkin and reached across the table to dab gently at Bailey's lips, causing her breath to catch.

How, she thought, could such a simple gesture evoke such intense, heated desire? She felt as though she were going up in flames, as though she would soon melt into a puddle and disappear.

William dropped the napkin onto the table, then drew his thumb lightly over Bailey's lips. She shivered at the tantalizing foray.

"There," he said, still leaning toward her. "All better."

He moved back in his chair, not a hint of a smile on his face.

"You're turning me inside out, Bailey Crandell," he said quietly, "and what I just saw in your eyes, on your face, tells me you feel the same way. There's more happening here than just lust or basic desire. There are emotions, too, emotions I've never experienced before. You know what I'm saying is true, don't you?''

"Yes," she said quietly, "I know it's more than just—" She paused and shook her head. "But I don't want to pursue it, William. I can't. All my energies, both physical and emotional, are centered on Sweet Fantasy. It takes that kind of focus for me to continue to succeed."

"Bailey, listen—"

She shook her head. "No. No, William, I really don't want to discuss this further." She looked at the dessert in front of her and saw that the ice cream had begun to melt and was running down the sides of the tall glass in less-than-appetizing rivers. "I guess I'm not hungry after all. I enjoyed the shopping trip, William, but I'm very tired, and I'd like to go home now, please."

He stared at her for a long moment, then pushed back his chair and got to his feet.

"All right, Bailey." His tone was pleasant and matter-of-fact, and there was no readable expression on his face. "We'll call it a night."

A little more than an hour later, Bailey crawled beneath the blankets on her bed and closed her eyes. The weary sound that escaped from her lips was more of a sob than a sigh.

William's behavior during the drive from The Ice Cream Parlor to where her car was parked at Sweet Fantasy had drained her of her last ounce of energy.

He had, she admitted, totally confused her, scrambled her brain. There she sat, while the hot fudge sundae turned to mush, telling him that she was aware that intense emotions were involved, along with the desire she felt for him. She had expected anger when she went on to say that whatever was happening between them was to be ignored because all she had, all she was, she must direct toward her business.

But instead, William had chattered away during the drive, just as chipper as could be. He'd told her which of the colored towels he'd purchased that night were to go in which bathroom in his house.

He was, he'd said, looking forward to their dinner date Saturday, and had decided to cook for her, and would include a tour of his new home—thrown in free.

At her car, William had kissed her deeply, told her to sleep well, then stood in the empty parking lot and watched her drive away.

Very strange, Bailey thought. Very, very strange.

She gave in to her bone-numbing fatigue and slept.

Across town, William was sprawled on his sofa, his fingers laced loosely on his chest, his legs stretched out in front of him.

Nice work, Lansing, he thought. His first reaction to Bailey's announcement that she refused to pursue what was happening between them had been to want to argue the point.

But at the last second he'd pulled back and re-grouped, quickly changing his strategy. And he'd rattled Miss Bailey Crandell, that was for darn sure.

Why was he doing this? he asked himself, causing his smug smile to switch to a frown. Bailey wasn't even close to The Perfect Wife he was seeking. She was career-oriented, not hearth-and-home. She spoke fondly of bonbons, not babies. She might like old-fashioned music, but she certainly wasn't enchanted by the lifestyle of bygone eras.

So why was he doing this?

Hell, he didn't know.

All that he was certain of was that Bailey Crandell had cast a spell over him, and until he figured out what he was going to do about it, he couldn't, wouldn't, just turn his back and walk away.

Five

Bailey stood in front of the long counter, which was matched in length by the mirror above it. She flicked a brush through her dark, slightly damp curls, then switched her gaze to Alice's reflection in the mirror. Alice stood next to her, applying fresh lipstick, unaware of Bailey's scrutiny.

Alice and William really did look alike, Bailey mused. It had been too hectic at the bazaar to take a thorough inventory of the pair.

They had the same dark hair, although Alice's was naturally curly. Alice's feminine version of William's rugged features made the sister absolutely lovely, while the brother was drop-dead handsome. The pussy-willow-gray eyes were there, and anyone would be able to tell that they were related.

"Oh, my aching body," Alice said, dusting blush over a cheek. "I put myself through this aerobics agony so I can have the luxury of the hot tub afterward. I'm beginning to think there's something wrong with that logic. The exercises have not gotten one iota easier in all these months."

When Bailey didn't reply, Alice looked questioningly at the younger woman's reflection in the mirror, then turned to face her.

"Hello?" Alice said. "Is my nose on upside down? Did one of my ears fall off?"

"What? Oh, I'm sorry. I was just marveling at how much you and William look alike."

"Yes, we do." Alice smiled brightly. "I guess whenever you see me, you'll think of William."

"Yes," Bailey said quietly, "I suppose I will."

"William is a great guy. Well, he's a tad stubborn and set in his ways, but most men are, in my opinion. William is so cute. Don't you think he's cute?"

"No. He's handsome, ruggedly handsome. That's far different from cute, Alice."

"I stand corrected," she said, managing to suppress a smile. "Anyway, William is very special." Her smile changed to a frown. "Well, I really do have to admit that his uniqueness, per se, is a royal pain in the tush at times."

"What do you mean?"

"This stand of his on not settling for less than his idea of an old-fashioned woman as his life's partner is so frustrating I could just scream. He refers to this elusive creature as The Perfect Wife. That's with capital letters, no doubt, like an official title. I've tried to get through to him that he's got to compromise a bit on the subject, or he'll end up alone and lonely. Does the man listen to me? Of course not. He just sets that jaw of his, and that's that."

"I don't know, Alice," Bailey said. "As strongly as William feels about it, I'm not sure that compromise is possible."

"That's a depressing thought. Maybe I'll just wring his neck so I don't have to worry about him."

"You two are very close. That's nice, it really is. I can remember wishing I had a brother or sister while I was growing up."

Alice laughed. "It guarantees you someone to squabble with."

"Alice, I was wondering if you might suggest a housewarming gift that I could give William. He is, after all, living in his brand-new house, and I'd like to take something with me to acknowledge the fact. I know the color schemes of the bathrooms, but beyond that I have no idea what he would need."

"Cut," Alice said, slicing one hand through the air. "You've totally lost me. You're going to William's new house? When? And why would you know the color of the bathrooms and nothing else about the place? Good grief, did you two have an in-depth discussion about the bathroom decor after Raymond and I left you in that restaurant the other night?"

"No." Bailey laughed, then began to place her makeup in a small zippered tote bag, averting her eyes from Alice's. "He came by Sweet Fantasy Monday for some hard candy to soothe his sore throat. Then Tuesday we went shopping for towels and what-have-you for the three bathrooms in his house."

"This is Thursday," Alice said. "Let's see. Oh, yes, I remember him saying he had a meeting on Wednesday night. Interesting. Carry on, Bailey. When are you scheduled to go to his house, and why?"

Bailey frowned. "The CIA could use you. I simply asked you for a suggestion for a housewarming gift."

"Surely you jest. You really didn't think you'd get away with that, did you? I want details, my dear, nitty-gritty details."

"You're nosy."

"It's in my job description as William's big sister. Don't stall, Bailey. You'll announce in a minute that you have to get to work and you can't chat further now. I'll follow you all the way to Sweet Fantasy if I have to. You can't hint at things, then clam up. My nervous system won't stand the strain."

Bailey smiled and shook her head. "You're terrible, and as stubborn as your brother. Okay, I give up. William invited me to have dinner at his house Saturday night. He's doing the cooking. Hence, a housewarming gift is in order. It's not a big deal, Alice."

Oh, ha, Bailey thought in the next instant. *Not a big deal?* Every time she envisioned being alone with William in his home for hours, she felt a flutter of heat course through her. She bounced back and forth between not wanting to go and counting the hours until she would be with him. The man was definitely driving her crazy.

"My, my," Alice said, "what a dreamy expression, Miss Crandell."

Bailey blinked. "Pardon me?"

"Nothing. I was just mumbling about something. Back to business. A housewarming gift. How about a coffee-table book? You know, one of those oversize volumes with gorgeous pictures of whatever."

"What kind of whatever?"

Alice squinted at the ceiling for a moment, then snapped her fingers and looked at Bailey again.

"Birds," Alice said. "William has had a fascination with birds since he was a boy. He's particularly enthralled by hummingbirds. He says it's rather... humbling—yes, that's the word he uses—to see something as tiny and delicate as a hummingbird survive in nature's arena and do it with such dignity and class."

"What a lovely thing to say," Bailey said, realizing she was alarmingly close to tears. "There are many facets to your brother, Alice."

"Indeed there are. The right woman would have the pleasure of discovering his depth. It would be like slowly unwrapping a present, a treasure, and revealing each fascinating layer.''

"The right woman? An old-fashioned woman, to be precise. The Perfect Wife.''

"Mmm . . .'' Alice frowned. "I'm back to wanting to wring William's neck. Well, I've got to dash. Have a super day, Bailey. Bye.''

"Goodbye,'' she said quietly as Alice left the room.

She leaned forward to peer in the mirror, convinced that the dark cloud she now felt hovering above her must surely be visible.

Business was brisk at Sweet Fantasy, and Bailey was glad to be assisted by Kris, one of the college students who worked at the shop.

At closing time, she said good-night to Kris, locked the front door behind her, flipped the sign over and headed for the rear area. As she entered the room, Deborah Crandell came in the back door.

Bailey raised her eyebrows in surprise at her mother's unexpected arrival. When Deborah sat down at the table, Bailey settled into the chair opposite her.

"Hello,'' Bailey said, smiling. "Fancy meeting you here. To what do I owe this honor, Mrs. Crandell?''

Deborah clasped her hands on top of the table and sat up straighter, squaring her shoulders.

"I wanted to talk to you, Bailey, and if you don't have any plans for this evening, I thought this might be a good time.''

"I was going shopping for a gift, but I can do that tomorrow night," she said slowly. She frowned, looking more intently at her mother. "Is something wrong? This obviously isn't going to be chitchat and gossip."

"Nothing is wrong, darling," Deborah said, smiling gently. "In fact, everything is very right." She paused a moment, gathering her thoughts. "Bailey, you're aware that I had an extremely difficult time after your father died. I was emotionally devastated, felt totally lost, with no sense of direction, or purpose. The role I'd had for decades was no longer there, and I didn't know what to do, or where I belonged."

Bailey nodded, her eyes riveted on Deborah's face. "Yes, I realize that, Mother. You were so unhappy. You'd devoted yourself to Dad, me, our home, and then suddenly it all changed."

"I will be eternally grateful to you, Bailey, for snatching me up by the britches and making a place for me, and Millie, here at the store."

"You're both wonderful employees. I couldn't ask for better. Sweet Fantasy met your and Millie's needs, just as it continually meets mine. I'm delighted that it all worked out so well for everyone."

"That's what I wanted to discuss with you tonight, dear."

"Oh?"

"Everything you said is true, but the time has come for me to look further. I'm ready, very eager, to add more to my life."

"More?" Bailey repeated, surprised. She glanced quickly around the room, then redirected her attention to her mother. "More than Sweet Fantasy?"

"Yes, more than Sweet Fantasy. Like your Pegasus, I want to spread my wings."

"But—" Bailey began. Then she stopped speaking, an incredulous expression on her face.

"Bailey, Millie and I are pooling our money and buying a motor home."

"What?" Bailey said, the word coming out in the form of a squeak.

"We've thoroughly enjoyed our little jaunts, such as the one to San Diego later this month. But we want to be in charge of where we go, what we see, how long we stay. We're going to, as they say, hit the road and see where it takes us."

"Dear heaven," Bailey whispered, "I . . . I don't believe this."

Deborah leaned forward, her eyes sparkling. "We're so excited, Bailey, we feel like young girls again. We'll have marvelous adventures, learn so much, enrich our lives. We both owe you a million thanks for making room for us here, but it's time to move on. We'll wait, of course, until you've hired and trained our replacements. Then, off we go. And that, my darling daughter, is what I wanted to talk to you about."

Bailey nodded absently, her mind racing.

She was already, she knew, on mental overload due to the turmoil in her mind regarding William. Now this.

What she had just heard from her mother was nearly too much to fully comprehend.

She felt as though her world, everything as she had known it to be, were crumbling into dust, leaving nothing familiar to cling to like a lifeline.

"Well," she said, forcing a smile, "I'm a tad stunned, but I wish you well, Mother. I hope you and Millie have a wonderful time."

"Oh, we will. We'll keep our homes, of course. Our first trip will be rather short, sort of a test run to work out the kinks. We'll have to plan carefully so we don't get caught in nasty winter weather back east." Deborah laughed. "You should see the lists that Millie and I have, the details we're checking and rechecking."

"That's good," Bailey said weakly. "It's very efficient."

"Well, I must be going," Deborah said, getting to her feet. She took one step toward the door, then stopped. She turned to look at Bailey again, a serious expression on her face. "Bailey, everyone grows and changes, or at least they should. You've devoted yourself to Sweet Fantasy. Have you ever considered the possibility that *you* might need more in your life now?"

"I don't have time, space, room, for anything else," she said, her voice rising. "Besides, *I* don't need more."

"Don't you?" Deborah said quietly. "Good night, my darling."

After Deborah left through the rear door, an oppressive silence hung over the room. Bailey leaned back in her chair and wrapped her hands around her elbows as a shiver coursed through her.

"I don't need more," she whispered.

But the softly spoken words seemed to bounce back at her from all directions, slamming against her with increasing force and volume.

She pressed shaking hands over her ears in a futile attempt to shut out the disturbing cacophony.

Stop it, she thought, dropping her hands back into her lap. Okay, so Sweet Fantasy was hers. Alone. It was just her... Bailey Crandell. She was proud of her accomplishments to date and of what she would continue to achieve. The shop was her purpose, her focus.

But...

It wasn't enough.

"Oh, Bailey," she said aloud, tears filling her eyes, "don't do this to yourself."

All those long, tedious hours, she thought frantically, all those hours she'd spent working for minimum wage, gathering her data, charting her life's course. Were they all for nothing?

But, dear heaven, as she pictured in her mind her future existence, pictured it as nothing more than herself and Sweet Fantasy, it was too cold, too empty, too lonely.

It wasn't enough.

Two tears slid down her cheeks.

"Yes, it *is* enough," she said, a desperate edge to her voice.

She was unsettled, she reasoned, had been thrown off kilter by having too much to handle at one time. But, darn it, the bottom line remained the same. Sweet Fantasy was her dream come true, the result of meticulous preparation, the place where all her physical and emotional energies *must* be directed in order to further nurture the ever-growing business.

Yes, that was how it was, had been for a long time, would remain far, far into the future. But as she viewed that future in her mind's eye, it was shrouded in an all-too-familiar dark cloud.

Bailey threw up her hands in a gesture of fatigue and defeat, folded her arms on the top of the table, lowered her head onto them and wept.

On Saturday night, Bailey stood before the full-length mirror that hung on the inside of her closet door, scrutinized her reflection, then nodded in approval.

The outfit wasn't fancy, she mused, but then, dinner at home called for simple but attractive. Raspberry-colored slacks, a pale pink string sweater and flat white sandals was appropriate attire. She'd given herself extra points for the raspberry toenail polish.

"Fine," she said aloud.

She closed the door, deciding she'd had quite enough of staring at her own image. If William knew she'd deliberated for half the day as to what to wear, she'd be mortified.

Due to the cost of establishing Sweet Fantasy, her wardrobe budget was very limited, each selection carefully chosen with mix-and-match in mind. So she'd mixed-and-matched for a ridiculous length of time, like an adolescent preparing for her first date.

With a cluck of self-disgust, she left the bedroom, turning out the light as she went. In the living room, she sat down, then was on her feet an instant later, wandering aimlessly around the room.

She stopped at one end table and ran a fingertip across the glossy brown-and-white-striped paper covering the coffee-table book about birds that she'd purchased as a housewarming gift for William. A large, shiny brown bow was perched on one edge.

The fact that there was no card accompanying the present caused her to roll her eyes as she remembered the hour she'd spent reading and rejecting a multitude of cards.

She sat down again on the sofa, took a deep breath, then let it out slowly.

Get it together, she told herself. The evening was going to be pleasant. She'd have a tour of William's new house, enjoy a nice dinner, then engage in interesting conversation. It was a run-of-the-mill date.

And that was such a blatant lie, her nose was going to grow like Pinocchio's.

There was nothing remotely run-of-the-mill about William, or the physical and emotional reactions she had to the man. She was a befuddled mess, feeling as though she were in the midst of a tangled maze of confusion that was holding her fast.

She had to remember, she *had* to, that there was no room in her life for a serious relationship. She had to remember that Sweet Fantasy *was* enough to make her feel fulfilled. She had to remember that William was seeking an old-fashioned stay-at-home bake-cookies-from-scratch woman. The Perfect Wife.

A knock sounded at the door, and Bailey jerked in surprise. She stood and tapped one fingertip on her forehead.

"Remember to remember," she muttered.

She crossed the room and opened the door, a bright smile on her face.

"Good evening, William," she said cheerfully. "Please come in."

Oh, good Lord, she thought. William Lansing in gray slacks and a black dress shirt open at the neck was a magnificent sight to behold. The black shirt accentuated the night-darkness of his thick hair, the gray depths of his eyes, the bronze tone of his tan.

Beautiful. He was so beautiful.

Her heart was beating a wild tattoo, and heat was thrumming through her as she drank in the sight of him.

What was it, she wondered hazily, that she was supposed to remember?

She closed the door and turned to face William, hoping her smile wasn't as wobbly as it now felt.

"Hello, Bailey," he said. He brushed his lips over hers, and she shivered. "You look lovely."

"Thank you. So do you."

"Bailey, you *did* look through the peephole in the door before you opened it, didn't you?"

Bailey frowned slightly for a second at the expected change of topic, then shrugged.

"No," she said. "I didn't. I was expecting you at seven o'clock, it was seven, so I took for granted it was you at the door." She shrugged again.

"Do you think all the villains take a coffee break at seven?"

"Villains?" she said, with a burst of laughter. "Real live villains, with flowing capes, black hats and skinny mustaches?"

"This is not meant to be funny," he said, his dark brows knitting in a frown. "A woman alone, without a man to protect her, needs to follow strict safety precautions at all times."

"A man to protect her? That's a rather Victorian-era attitude, William. Women today are perfectly capable of taking care of themselves."

"Ha!" he said, his voice rising. "You didn't even peek out your peephole."

A bubble of laughter escaped from Bailey's lips, and she was unable to smother the smile that followed.

"That sounds rather risqué," she said, her blue eyes dancing with merriment. "Shall we go? Or do you want to holler at me some more first?"

He started to retort, then stopped. A slow smile crept onto his lips, then widened into a grin.

"Okay," he said, raising both hands in a gesture of peace. "I'll give it a rest—for now. Dinner awaits, ma'am. I'm changing into chef mode."

She wished he'd give the knock-'em-dead smile a rest, Bailey thought. That smile was sinful, and it caused funny flutters to tingle down her spine. In fact, William Lansing, from head to toe, should be declared against the law.

"Bailey?"

"Oh. Yes, I almost forgot. I have something for you." She moved around him to pick up the present. "This is a housewarming gift. Alice helped me decide what to get you." She held it out to him.

William looked directly into Bailey's eyes for a long moment. His gaze was intense, but she was unable to decipher its meaning. He finally switched his attention to the gift and took it from her.

"Thank you very much," he said, looking at the package. "May I sit down and open it?"

"Oh, yes, of course."

He sat down on the sofa, then looked up at Bailey, who hadn't moved. She walked around the coffee table and settled onto the cushion next to him. He began to unwrap the present slowly. Very slowly.

"Ohhh..." Bailey finally said with a moan. "You're one of those. I can't stand it. Tear off the paper, William. Rip it to shreds. Cut to the chase."

He chuckled. "Nope." The smile that had accompanied the chuckle faded, and when he turned his head to look at her, his expression was serious. "There's pleasure to be found in anticipation, Bailey."

He visually traced each of her features with an expression that was so blatantly sensual and so incredibly male that Bailey nearly forgot to breathe. When his smoldering gaze lingered on her lips, she could hear the rapid tempo of her heart echoing in her ears.

"Anticipation," he said, looking directly into her eyes again. His voice was low, with a gritty quality to it. "It certainly does hold its own appeal. Don't you agree?"

"Oh, my, yes," she said dreamily.

William leaned toward her, then flicked his tongue over her lips. Bailey's breath caught as spiraling heat thrummed low within her.

If he didn't kiss her, she thought hazily, *really* kiss her, she was going to die on the spot. Oh, dear heaven, what this man did to her...

William slipped one hand to the nape of her neck, then captured her mouth, parting her lips to stroke her tongue with his own.

Bailey's lashes drifted down as she savored his taste, the feel of his sensuous lips, his aroma of soap and woodsy after-shave. Her tongue met his eagerly, dueling, dancing, heightening the swirling, heated desire that was rapidly consuming her.

Anticipation. William's mind hummed. The thought of kissing Bailey had tantalized him that entire day. Now he *was* kissing her, and it was ecstasy.

But he wanted more.

Anticipation? Lord, the mental image of making love with Bailey was enough to fling him to the edge of his control.

Never before had he desired a woman as he did Bailey. Never before had he experienced such a fierce sense of possessiveness and protectiveness. Never before had a woman claimed his mind in the day and invaded his dreams at night, the way Bailey did.

He was on fire, going up in flames of passion, wanting, needing, Bailey Crandell.

He tore his mouth from hers and took a ragged breath, willing his aroused body back under his command.

Bailey slowly opened her eyes. "Your birds," she whispered.

"My what?" he said, shaking his head slightly. "My who?"

Bailey blinked, bringing herself back to reality from the misty place she'd floated to.

"The book," she said, her voice not quite steady. "Your birds. The housewarming gift."

William looked at the present that rested on his thighs. "Oh." He slid his fingers along the edge of the paper, and a moment later lifted the book free. "Fantastic! This is great, Bailey. Look at that hummingbird on the cover. Beautiful. I have a thing for hummingbirds." He flipped through the glossy pages. "This is very, very nice. Thank you."

"You're welcome. I really can't take credit for it, though, because Alice told me you like birds, especially hummingbirds."

He met her gaze. "But you picked it out, wrapped it, gave it to me. That's special. *You're* special. This book will have a place of honor on my coffee table." He paused. "I'd kiss you further to express my thanks, but I don't think that would be a good idea right now. I want you very much, Bailey, and I believe that you want me. I also believe, just as I said the other night, that there are emotions, important emotions, involved here, too."

"William, I—"

"No, please, don't say anything. I realize that you're convinced that you don't have room, time, whatever, in your life for more than Sweet Fantasy. But I *am* in your life, Bailey. Think about it. Come on, let's go. I promised you dinner, and dinner you shall have, my lady."

My lady, Bailey's mind echoed as they left the apartment. Didn't that have a lovely ring to it? My lady. William's lady. His. Bailey Crandell was William Lansing's lady, and William Lansing was most definitely in the midst of Bailey Crandell's life.

No!

Stop it, she scolded herself. The minute she came into close proximity to William, her mind went prancing down fairy-tale lane.

All right, Bailey, she mentally rambled on, here's the program. During the hours of the evening ahead, she'd be in a Cinderella mind-set. She'd enjoy William's company and, yes, his kiss and his touch. There was no harm in that, as long as she remembered that at midnight she had to return to reality.

Her reality was Sweet Fantasy.

But oh, dear heaven, in her mind's eye her reality was lonely.

Six

During the tour of William's house, Bailey quickly ran out of adjectives to describe how fantastic it was. She was simply going to smile and nod, she informed him, which resulted in him giving her a hard, fast kiss.

William's pride of ownership was delightful, and his enthusiasm was infectious. Attention had been given to the smallest details, which William pointed out with wide sweeps of his arms and a smile on his face.

The house was enormous and had been built in the exclusive Camelback Mountain area. There were four bedrooms, the master suite being at the opposite end of the house from the other bedrooms. Flagstone fireplaces had been constructed in the living room, family room and master bedroom.

An entertainment center covered one entire wall of the family room, and held, it appeared to Bailey, every type of equipment available for leisure-time activities. Speakers connected to the stereo had been mounted on a wall of each room in the house, with a volume control above the light switch.

The carpeting throughout was plush, chocolate brown, and the furniture was obviously expensive but purchased for use, not show. Although not all the rooms had furniture, what was there was dark wood, with material that would wear well.

In the kitchen, which was bigger than Bailey's entire apartment, William had demonstrated how the safety catches on the cupboards and drawers worked. Bailey listened absently, firming up in her mind a thought that had been taking shape during the tour.... William's home had most definitely been designed for a family. All that was missing was The Perfect Wife, followed by The Perfect Children.

"We'll be eating here in the kitchen," William was saying. "As you saw, I don't have any furniture for the dining room yet. Why don't you sit down there at the table, I'll pour you a glass of wine, and we can chat while I'm cooking?"

Bailey nodded and settled into one of the captain's chairs at the large oval table. Two places had been set with stoneware dishes, clever glasses that looked like canning jars, and flatware with handles that picked up one of the colors from the plates. White candles in square holders of highly polished dark wood awaited a match.

"As I have run out of ways to say it, William," Bailey said, "your home is magnificent. This table is lovely, too. You have a flair for decorating."

"Not really." He brought her the promised wine, then began to chop up vegetables for a salad. "I studied a stack of books to get ideas. Next up is to wallpaper one of the extra bedrooms. That will be a real challenge."

Bailey propped one elbow on the table and rested her chin on her hand.

"It still amazes me," she said. "that you didn't hire somebody to do it for you. I would think that being an investment broker would be a challenge enough in itself."

William nodded. "It was for a long time, but the spark has gone out of it. I do a good job for my clients, but the excitement, the sense of fulfillment I have, stems from working on this house. I still want to have a pool put in, but I have some investigating to do on that. My concern is safety first, then design."

"William, this house was built with a focus on family, wasn't it?"

He glanced over at her, then returned to his chopping chores. "Absolutely. I have a lot to do here, but eventually, it will be a family-oriented home. Have you ever hung wallpaper?"

"Me? No."

"It might be fun to attempt it together. What do you think?"

Hanging wallpaper would be fun? Bailey thought. It sounded like hard work, a messy project. Did she want to hang wallpaper? Not really. Did being with William hold appeal? Oh, yes.

"Bailey?"

"I'm game, but don't expect expertise. I don't have the foggiest idea how to even start."

"I have a book of instructions. I also have a book on how to make salad dressing." He peered at a book on the counter. "The chicken has been on slow-bake in the oven for just about long enough. The vegetables are in the pan with the chicken. I'm really getting a handle on this cooking stuff."

"My motto is, if it can't be microwaved, it's not on the menu."

"Oh."

"I don't have time, energy or inclination to cook, decorate, or bake cookies from scratch," she said.

Good grief, she thought, that had sounded defensive. William was just chatting, sharing, not pinning her to the wall on the issue. Maybe the edge in her voice stemmed from the sudden knot in her stomach at the glaring truth that she wasn't remotely close to William's idea of The Perfect Wife.

"Oh, you never know," he said, bringing the salad to the table. He looked directly into Bailey's eyes. "People change. If someone would have told me a couple of years ago that I would get a kick out of learning to cook, decorate a house, the whole nine yards, I would have said they were nuts. Now? I enjoy all this far more than my chosen career. I still have lots of plans for this place, and I'm eager to keep at it.''

"That's nice," she said, with a weary little sigh.

"I have a ways to go before this house is ready for a family, but someday—" He didn't finish his sentence. The timer went off, interrupting him. "We eat, my lady."

No. Bailey thought, feeling the dark cloud taking shape above her, she wasn't his lady, and never would be. Well, that was fine. Sure it was. She was Cinderella at the ball for now. Besides, it was becoming obvious that William intended to have The Perfect House before he selected The Perfect Wife. So for now there was no problem.

William removed the baking pan from the oven and began to transfer the chicken and vegetables onto a platter.

Bailey liked the house, he mused. He was certain of that. But he also had to acknowledge that she apparently had no natural instincts for domesticity, nor hidden yearnings to be a homemaker. She was one-hundred-percent career-oriented.

That would not be disturbing, if he'd kept her in the casual-dating category, but she was becoming more than that to him. What exactly his new and startling emotions meant, he wasn't certain, but there was nothing casual about whatever it was that was happening between them.

Hell, he thought, what a mess. He'd built this house for a family. When the house was finally completed as he intended it, he wanted a wife, children, so that the house became a home. Well, he still had many projects to complete before the place was wife-ready. Maybe, just maybe, Bailey would get caught up in the sense of fulfillment of creating a home out of a house.

Was that what he wanted? Were the strange emotions he felt for her the first stirrings of love, of falling in love, of being in love?

Ah, hell, he didn't know!

Bailey leaned back in her chair, splayed one hand over her stomach and sighed.

"William," she said, smiling, "I'm stuffed. That was a delicious dinner. The caramel custard for dessert did me in, though. I may not move for a month."

"I'm glad you enjoyed it," he said, matching her smile. "Would you like some coffee?"

"No, thank you, not right now. I insist on helping you with the dishes. I've been pampered and waited upon, but enough is enough."

"Nope. This is my first attempt at cooking for a guest, and I'll see it through to its proper end. Besides, loading a dishwasher isn't all that tough." He got to his feet. "You stay put."

"You talked me into it," she said with a laugh.

As William cleared the table and tended to the cleanup chores, Bailey watched him from beneath her lashes.

It had been a lovely dinner, she mused. Not only had the food been tasty, but the conversation had been lively, interesting, one topic flowing into the next with comfortable ease.

William began to hum an indiscernible tune as he filled the dishwasher.

He was really enjoying himself, Bailey thought, and the startling thing was that he looked, well...right, moving about his kitchen. His enthusiasm for what he was doing enhanced his masculinity, instead of diminishing it, even though he was working in what might be considered by some to be a woman's arena.

Oh, yes, William Lansing was all man, no matter what he was doing. Cinderella could keep her Prince Charming, Bailey decided. William would suit Bailey fine, thank you very much.

Just until midnight, she quickly tacked on. Yes, she'd like to continue to see William until midnight tonight and the days that followed, but she mustn't forget the Cinderella principle: whatever she might share with William was only temporary. The reality, the focus, the purpose, of her life was her work.

William wiped off the counters, flipped on the dishwasher, then told Bailey he'd be back in a minute. A few moments later, a lilting Strauss waltz could be heard coming from the speakers mounted high on the kitchen wall.

William returned and extended his hand to Bailey.

"May I have this dance?" he said.

Cinderella, eat your heart out, Bailey thought, as she placed her hand in William's.

He led her into the empty dining room, where the chandelier had been dimmed to a soft glow and the lovely music filled the air. As he drew her into his arms, Bailey sighed with pleasure, marveling at how perfectly they fitted together.

In spite of the thick carpeting, they seemed to float around the room as the waltz ended and another began.

Oh, William, Bailey thought dreamily. He was making her feel as though she were, indeed, a princess at a ball, so beautiful, feminine, cherished. Her senses were heightened to a nearly painful intensity by the nearness of William's magnificent body. Desire was building within her like an ember being coaxed into a raging flame.

Bailey, William's mind hummed. She was heaven itself in his arms, felt as delicate as the enchanting hummingbird on the cover of the book she had given him. That gift meant so much to him. He would keep it on the coffee table, and he would keep Bailey in his arms, just as she was now.

Ah, Bailey, he thought, pressing her even closer against him. Her breasts were crushed to his chest, she was nestled to the cradle of his hips, her floral aroma was sweet, tantalizing, and he wanted her with every breath in his body. He was aroused, aching. He was on fire, burning with need for Bailey.

William stopped dancing, Bailey looked up at him, and then his mouth melted over hers. The invisible threads, the now-familiar sensuous web, spun around them, creating a warm cocoon where only they, together, could exist.

Bailey's heart was racing and her legs were trembling. Heat was swirling throughout her, causing her breasts to become heavy and pulsing desire to throb low within her. Raw, stark desire shone in the smoky gray depths of William's eyes, and her heart quickened even more as her lashes drifted down.

She was edging past the point of sensible reasoning, she mused hazily. The moment, this night, was over-shadowing all logical thoughts of tomorrow, and the recriminations she might fling around herself like a heavy, uncomfortable cloak.

She was only Cinderella for a short length of time. She had no room, no space, in her life for a special man.

She knew that.

William Lansing was dangerous, because he'd had a tremendous emotional and physical impact on her from the moment they met.

She knew that.

That she desired William with an intensity that was nearly shattering meant that walking away from him once they'd made love would cause her to cry in the dark, lonely hours of the night.

She knew that.

But she didn't care.

There was only now, and William.

The kiss was an explosion of wondrous sensations. Kissing William Lansing was pure ecstasy.

And she knew that.

Their tongues met in the sweet darkness of Bailey's mouth, heightening their passion.

William raised his head to draw in a rough breath, then captured Bailey's lips once again, his control slipping beyond his reach.

"Bailey," he said, his voice a hoarse whisper, "I want to make love with you."

She smiled. It was a soft, gentle, womanly smile that spoke more eloquently than words could have.

Encircling her shoulders with one arm, he led her from the dining room and down the hall to the master bedroom. He threw back the blankets on the bed, then snapped on a small lamp on one of the nightstands that cast a rosy glow over the large room.

Then he drew her close, wrapping his arms around her, holding her fast, as though he would never again let her go. Finally he eased her away just enough to meet her gaze, to see the same desire he knew shone in his eyes mirrored in hers.

A groan rumbled deep in his chest as he reveled in the knowledge that Bailey wanted him with the same incredible intensity as he wanted her. He wove his fingers through her dark, silken curls, and then his mouth claimed hers in a kiss that was searing, urgent, hungry.

He dropped his hands to slide them under her sweater, then up and over the satiny smoothness of her back. His hands moved forward, and he filled his palms with the bounty of her breasts, his thumbs stroking nipples to taut buttons beneath the wispy lace of her bra. A purr of pleasure caught in Bailey's throat.

William broke the kiss, then placed one hand on her cheek. She turned her head to kiss his palm lightly. It was such a simple gesture, a large male hand gently resting on the soft skin of a feminine cheek, yet to Bailey it was precious, tender, a quiet pause in the raging passion that consumed them. Tears misted her eyes.

"Bailey?" William said, a frown instantly on his face. "What's wrong?"

"Nothing," she said, a lovely smile forming on her lips. "No, no, William, there's nothing wrong." Because this was so very right. This was their night, perhaps the only one they would have, and she would never regret this decision. "Honestly."

He drew her into his arms and kissed her deeply once more, and then they both stepped back and shed their clothes. The rosy glow of the light seemed to flow over them like a waterfall, accentuating the body that was gently curved and soft as ivory velvet, and the body that was tautly muscled, tanned, with dark curls covering a chest broad and strong.

Bailey's gaze swept over William, etching each magnificent detail indelibly on her mind. He was fully aroused, and a shiver of anticipation swept through her as she saw all that he would bring to her. She looked into his eyes again.

"You're beautiful," she whispered. "You're such a beautiful man, William."

He smiled. "That's the word I was about to use to describe you, Bailey. *You* are beautiful, like a statue carved from flawless marble."

"No, I'm a woman, and at this moment I can't think of anything else I would wish to be. I'm the feminine counterpart to your masculinity, and I ache with the want of you."

"Bailey, I—" A tightness gripped his throat, choking off his words.

He lifted her into his arms and kissed her before placing her in the center of the bed, then stretching out next to her. He rested on one forearm, his other hand splayed on the flat plane of her stomach.

He met her gaze for a long moment, then lowered his head to draw the sweet flesh of one of her breasts into his mouth.

Bailey gasped as heated sensations exploded throughout her. The rhythmic suckling of William's mouth on her sensitive breast caused a matching pulse to beat deep and low within her.

When he moved to the other breast, a near-sob caught in her throat as her passion flared even more, reaching a height such as she had never before known. She tossed her head restlessly on the pillow, control lost, want and need reigning supreme.

"William, please," she said, her voice seeming to come from some faraway place. "Please. I want you . . . now. Please."

"Yes." His voice was hoarse with passion.

He kissed her deeply, then moved over her, catching his weight on his arms, hovering above her, as he looked yet again at her lovely flushed cheeks and her expressive eyes, which were nearly a smoky blue with the evidence of her want of him.

His muscles quivering from forced restraint, he entered her, the moist heat that welcomed and received him nearly flinging him over the edge of control.

Slowly, slowly, he moved deep within her, savoring the sensations rocketing within him, relishing the pain of need as he anticipated the ecstasy of release.

But Bailey's pleasure must come first, he thought, sweat glistening on his body. This night, this joining, was so important. It had to be perfect for his Bailey.

Bailey forced herself to concentrate, to push aside for a moment the sensuous mist clouding her mind. She became aware of the trembling of William's muscles, of his sweat-soaked skin, of his labored breathing. She could feel his manhood deep within her, and his stillness as he waited for her body to adjust to the size and power of him.

She had never, she knew, felt so cherished, so special, had never been the recipient of a gift such as the one William was giving her. Her heart seemed to be about to burst beneath her breast. It was overflowing with emotions and messages concealed by the mist that once again floated over her.

William, her mind, body and heart hummed. That was where her focus belonged now, centered on William. William, who had filled her with the essence of

himself, and now trembled from the effort of the tight
control he was exerting. He was giving, and giving, and
now it was time for her to give, as well.

"William . . ." she whispered, then raised her hips.

"Bailey, don't," he said through clenched teeth.
"Wait, go easy. I don't want to hurt you. I—"

She slid her hands sensuously down his slick back,
feeling the muscles bunch and move enticingly beneath
her palms. Again she lifted her hips, increasing the
pressure of her hands.

William groaned as the last thread of his control
snapped. He began to move within her, increasing the
tempo with each thrust—faster, harder, deeper. Bailey
matched his rhythm in harmony, as though the two of
them had been specially created to be partners in this
age-old dance.

The sensuous mist hovering around Bailey began to
glitter and shimmer like a million exquisite diamonds.
She clung tightly to William's shoulders as she began to
feel the sensation of being swept up and away, flying
like Pegasus, being flung closer and closer to the glorious place that was sparkling a welcome.

Closer and closer, then closer still.

William thundered within Bailey, each thrust bringing greater pleasure as she matched his wild cadence,
beat for beat. Bailey's name echoed in his mind and
heart in concert with the tempo of their bodies, which
were meshed as one entity.

Never, he thought hazily, had lovemaking been so meaningful on the emotional plane, so pleasurable on the physical.

"William..." Bailey said, pressing her fingertips even harder into his shoulders. "Oh, dear heaven—William!"

She burst into the midst of the diamond-like maze as spasms of pure, rich pleasure rushed through her in waves, like rolling rapids. Her body tightened around him, pulling him deeper still, as though urging him to join her in the place of ecstasy. A heartbeat later, he did.

"Bailey!"

With one last thrust, he flung his head back and closed his eyes as his life's force passed from him into her. The release was exquisite, powerful, bringing a sigh from his lips, and draining the last ounce of energy from his body.

He collapsed against her, resting his head next to hers on the pillow. She wrapped her arms around his back. They drifted slowly from the glittering place, and the brilliant lights dimmed, then faded away, as they returned to reality.

But reality, too, was bliss.

They were sexually sated, still entwined, and it was only William's growing concern that he was too heavy for Bailey that caused him to stir, then speak, breaking the contentment-filled silence.

"I'll crush you," he said, moving carefully off her.

He pulled the blankets up over them, then settled on his side close to her, one arm across her waist.

"Bailey," he said quietly, "you're wonderful. What we shared was wonderful."

"Yes," she said, tangling her fingers in the moist hair on his chest. "Yes, it was. Beautiful. You made me feel very special."

"You *are* special, but you gave me just as much in return, holding nothing back." He paused. "Thank you, Bailey. Maybe that sounds like a strange, corny thing to say, but I mean it sincerely. Thank you."

An achy sensation gripped Bailey's throat, making the presence of threatening tears known, and making it impossible for her to speak. She kept her gaze riveted on William's chest, afraid of the emotion that might be evident on her face, or in her eyes. An emotion that she herself could not clearly identify.

Thank you, Bailey, her mind echoed. What an incredibly tender, beautiful, meaningful thing for William to have said. He was so comfortable with his masculinity that he had no qualms about saying something romantic, something straight from his heart. Many men might have decided that expressing such a thing would cause them to be too vulnerable, but not William Lansing. No, not William. Thank you, Bailey. Oh, how she would cherish those words.

"I'll always remember this night, William, and what we shared."

"There will be many more nights like this one."

"No," she said softly. "No, William, this was our night, *ours,* but it can't happen again."

William propped himself up on one forearm to enable him to look directly into her eyes.

"That doesn't make sense," he said, a frown knitting his brows. "This wasn't just sex, we made love. There's a big difference between the two. Something is happening here that can't be ignored. You know what I'm saying is true."

"Yes, I *do* know that," she said, her voice rising. "Nothing like this, like you, has ever happened to me before. It's beautiful and rare. But in the next instant I have to face the fact that whatever this is between us might be powerful enough to pull me from the path where I belong, from the course I've charted for my life."

"Bailey—"

"Yes," she said interrupting him. "I'm Bailey Crandell, owner of Sweet Fantasy. I can't allow anything to cause me to forget who I am and where I belong. I have to concentrate totally on—"

"Sweet Fantasy," he said, his frown deepening. "It comes first with you."

"Not first, as though there's a list with other things on it. Sweet Fantasy is the entire list. When I give it what it has to have, there's nothing left over."

Bailey brushed her fingers across his cheek. He didn't say anything.

"I came here tonight as Cinderella, knowing this was stolen time. If you feel that was unfair to you, I apologize. But I made no promises. I thought perhaps we could go further than just tonight, as long as I remembered that the clock would eventually strike, as it did for Cinderella, and the fantasy would end. But—'' She stopped speaking and shook her head.

''But?''

''What we shared was so wonderful, so... I can't run the risk, don't you see? I have plans for Sweet Fantasy. My dream didn't end the day I opened for business. I want to do more, work toward having a delivery service, like a florist, but with gift baskets of candy instead of flowers, and all sorts of other things. I care for you, I truly do, but I don't know how to work all this out. Oh, William, please don't make this more difficult than it is.''

William looked directly into her eyes for a long moment before he spoke again. ''All right, Bailey,'' he said slowly.

''Then you *do* understand.''

''Whoa...'' he said, raising his hand. ''You're misinterpreting my acquiescence. What I actually meant was, 'All right, Bailey—for now.' This discussion is temporarily on hold. Oh, and our wallpapering project is still on.''

''But—''

''Shh,'' he said. ''This is our night, remember?''

Then his mouth captured hers.

Much later, Bailey went into the bathroom and began to dress, performing by rote as she concentrated on her jumbled thoughts.

She felt torn in two, she realized, with half of her going in one direction, the other half in another.

One part was in a firm mind-set, as it had always been, the focus and purpose of her existence centered on Sweet Fantasy, and the continued growth and success of her business.

But the other half? That was an entirely different story. The lovemaking shared with William had been so exquisitely beautiful it defied description.

It had seemed so right, so natural, to see him above her, passion evident in his beautiful gray eyes, to mesh her body with his, to become one with him.

Bailey sighed.

She was, she knew, terribly confused. She had stated her stand firmly, even outlining her future plans for Sweet Fantasy, yet William was still causing her to examine issues that she had not questioned since determining the course of her life. She had succumbed to his sensual power, which had caused rational thought and practical reason to be swept away.

Oh, dear, she thought, what did all these new and unsettling physical and emotional upheavals mean, *really* mean? While William was staking his claim to her thoughts in the day and her dreams at night, was he also sneaking up and inching toward having a tight hold on her heart, as well?

"No," she said aloud. "I simply won't allow that to happen."

She finished dressing as quickly as possible, combed her hair, then gripped the edge of the sink and drew a deep breath. She exhaled slowly, then leaned closer to the mirror.

Heavenly days, she thought, it showed. There was a rosy flush on her cheeks and a lovely glow in her eyes, both of which announced like a brilliant neon sign that she had taken part in glorious lovemaking.

If only there were other messages there for her to read so easily. Her inner turmoil and confusion were growing with every passing minute.

She knew, darn it, she *knew,* that she should walk out of this house *and* out of William's life, right now.

And she was also acutely aware that the mere image in her mind of doing that caused the ever-famous dark cloud to hover over her once again.

"Oh, Bailey..." she said to her reflection in the mirror. "What are you doing?"

She could *not* have a serious relationship with William Lansing. They were all wrong for each other, their goals too different. Yet she could *not* fade into the sunset and forget that he existed.

"Well, great," she said with a snort of self-disgust.

She had told William that she wished to go home now, that the night, the Cinderella night, was over. He'd moved off the bed and started to dress without argument. She was going to crawl into her own bed at her apartment and sleep, sleep, sleep.

An hour later, William reentered his house and walked slowly toward the master bedroom. He sat down on the edge of the bed and narrowed his eyes in concentration.

The drive to Bailey's apartment had taken place in total silence. He'd kissed her deeply at her door, said he'd see her soon, then waited until he heard the lock click into place after she went inside.

That woman was going to change his life irrevocably, he mused. How he knew that, he wasn't certain, but he was sure it was true. Did this knowledge, coming from a source unknown, mean that Bailey was the one he had been searching for? Was he destined to fall in love with her?

Fall in love with Bailey, he mentally repeated. Bailey Crandell of Sweet Fantasy. Bailey, who had not a job, but a career, a tremendous challenge that demanded all her concentration and energy.

If he did, actually did, fall in love with Bailey, would he end up with nothing, have only memories, empty arms and loneliness to face in a bleak future?

He had a choice. He could decide right there and then that Sweet Fantasy was too great an opponent, an unbeatable foe, and move on down the road on his mission to find the The Perfect Wife of his dreams.

Or he could dig in, hold fast, discover as time passed just how deep his feelings for Bailey would become, then fight for her like hell if he did, indeed, come to love her.

Choice A. Choice B.

The image of Bailey flickered in William's mind's eye, and he saw that satiny skin that had the delicate hue of a sun-kissed peach. He could actually smell the aroma of her light floral cologne and feel her soft, dark curls sift through his fingers. The remembrance of meshing his body with hers, of making love with Bailey, caused heat to once again churn low in his body.

Choice A. Choice B.

No contest. He was now committed to a mission of discovery. He'd find the answers to questions, and keep in touch with his inner voice.

He could only hope that at the end of his physical and emotional journey he wouldn't find himself alone and lonely, wondering how to glue back together the zillion pieces of his shattered heart.

A smile tugged at his lips, then blossomed into a grin.

Bailey had been emotionally unsettled tonight. Excellent. She hadn't said no when he announced that they'd go ahead with their plans to wallpaper together, to make it a project they'd share. He was determined to find the answers to his questions regarding his feelings for Bailey Crandell.

He'd bet his last ten dollars that Bailey would pass the remainder of the night sifting and sorting through the jumble in her mind. She was going to spend the following hours thinking, and thinking, and thinking....

She had to stop thinking, Bailey told herself for the umpteenth time. She was exhausted and wished only to sleep with no disturbing dreams intruding on her slumber.

She yanked the blankets to her chin and squeezed her eyes tightly closed. Three seconds later, her eyes popped open again.

"Blast," she said to the empty room. "William Lansing, would you kindly leave me be?"

When she finally slept, she had a chilling nightmare. She was standing in her shop, held in place by an invisible force, watching as William methodically consumed every ounce of candy in the store.

Sweet Fantasy was no more.

Seven

—

In her apartment the next afternoon, a tired and extremely grumpy Bailey yanked the vacuum-cleaner cord from the electrical socket with more force than was necessary.

The sudden silence of the machine revealed the shrill ringing of the telephone. She snatched up the receiver and mumbled a less-than-cordial greeting.

"Bailey?"

"William?" She sank onto the sofa, aware that the tempo of her heart had increased at the mere sound of his voice. She rolled her eyes in self-disgust.

"I was afraid you weren't there," William said. "I let the phone ring at least twenty times."

"I was vacuuming and didn't hear it."

"You should get an answering machine. That way a person would know that you're not at home. When a phone rings and rings, it evokes scenarios of your being sick, or hurt, needing help. I was really starting to panic."

Bailey frowned. "I do *not* need an answering machine. Besides, I'd never remember to turn it on when I started vacuuming. William, this is a ridiculous conversation."

"Oh. Right. Listen, I'm calling from the airport. One of my staff members had an appointment with an out-of-state client, but Kathy—that's the staff member—has the flu, so I'm taking her place. I'm not happy about it, believe me, but...I should be back Friday night, or Saturday morning at the latest."

"Oh," she said. She'd miss him. The fact had slammed against her with such force, she'd had to catch her breath.

"They're calling my plane. Bailey, plan on dinner out Saturday night. All right? Then Sunday we'll tackle the wallpaper. I have to run. Say yes."

"Yes, but—"

"Fantastic. I'll be thinking about you. Bye."

"But—" she repeated, then realized she was speaking to the dial tone. "Your train, Bailey Crandell," she said to no one, "is not stopping at all the stations."

Why, why, why, had she agreed to William's plans for the weekend? She should have said no, should have put as much time and distance between them as possible, before she was drawn deeper and deeper into the exciting, sensual, confusing, dangerous space that surrounded William Lansing.

The following days seemed endless. Bailey told herself that her gloomy mood was due to fatigue resulting from not sleeping well night after night, and from the unusually busy days at Sweet Fantasy. The fact that she didn't buy her own story for one second did not improve her deteriorating mood.

She did, indeed, miss William, but it was the intensity of that yearning to see him, the glaring void in her life because he wasn't there, that caused her growing despair.

What that meant on an emotional plane, she refused to address. She simply didn't have the fortitude yet to get in touch with herself and deal with what an inner dialogue would reveal.

At closing time on Thursday, Bailey stood in the back room of Sweet Fantasy, with the telephone pressed to her ear. Her mother, she knew, would see to the locking up of the front door.

"Yes. I'm still here," Bailey said into the receiver, as Deborah came into the rear area. "I was beginning to think you'd put me on hold and forgotten about me.... You're kidding. How could that have happened? I ordered those baskets nearly six weeks ago, with a specified delivery date, and you're saying . . ."

She squeezed the bridge of her nose, closed her eyes for a moment, and shook her head.

"Yes, of course, I realize that mistakes can happen in any business.... Well, that's cutting it close, but it will have to do.... All right. Yes, I understand. Fine. Thank you. Goodbye."

She replaced the receiver. "Damn."

"Problem?" Deborah asked, sitting down at the table.

Bailey crossed the room and sank onto the chair opposite her mother. "A definite glitch, Mother." She sighed wearily. "Do you remember how pleased I was when we got the order for thirty baskets to be made up for Mrs. Chamberlain? She's having a lawn party to celebrate her husband's fiftieth birthday?"

"I certainly do remember. That was a feather in your cap, to say the least."

"Well, the feather just flew the coop. Mrs. Chamberlain chose the basket she wanted from the album I showed her. I ordered thirty, with a hold to deliver them today. This is Thursday, so I'd have plenty of time to pack the shelf goods in the baskets, then come in early Sunday to finish up with the perishables."

Bailey paused for a moment, Deborah waited, then said, "So?"

"The chocolate cups have arrived safely, the whipped cream is in the refrigerator, so I was going to fill the cups with cream Sunday morning. The air-conditioning in here would keep the cream cool enough, and the Chamberlains' son is picking up the baskets at noon. Mrs. Chamberlain said they have three refrigerators, so they'll have no problem with the whipped cream spoiling. Anyway, we had it all worked out, down to the smallest detail."

"And?"

"No baskets," Bailey said, folding her arms on the top of the table. "That was the supplier on the phone. Somehow my order was processed with the wrong delivery date. He's going to load up the baskets now, but they won't be here until Saturday. He's giving me a ten-percent discount because of the inconvenience, which is very nice, but it doesn't solve the time crunch at this end."

"You know I'll come in and help you, Bailey."

"You certainly will not. You and Millie are leaving at dawn Saturday on the bus tour down to San Diego, and you won't be back until late Monday night. You've been looking forward to it for weeks, and I won't hear of you changing your plans."

"But..."

Bailey smiled. "Ignore me, Mother. I'm just pouting like a pro over this basket-delivery mix-up. I'll work extra hours, and the birthday picnic will go on as scheduled. Kris can help me between customers on Saturday, too. Put the whole thing out of your mind."

"Well..."

"It will be fine, Mother."

"Well," Deborah said, getting to her feet. "I know better than to argue with you when you get that stubborn look in your eyes. Besides, you've obviously thought of how to adapt to the scheduling change."

"Absolutely. I'm a dynamite organizer."

Deborah smiled. "That you are. You run this business like a captain at the helm of a smooth-sailing ship. In fact, I'd say that because of that there's room in your life for more than just Sweet Fantasy."

"Correct. The 'more' is phase two of Sweet Fantasy."

"The delivery service," her mother said, her smile vanishing. "Oh, darling, your ambition and willingness to work hard are admirable, and I'm very proud of you. All I'm asking is that you remember how lost I was when I no longer had the only role I'd known for so many years."

"I appreciate your concern, Mother, but my circumstances are entirely different. I have plans, dreams, goals, for Sweet Fantasy, and since it's a business, it will be there for as long as I devote myself to its continued success. I fully intend to do that."

Deborah started to reply but changed her mind and shook her head. "All right, Bailey. I've said my piece. You're old enough to live your life without a nagging mother fussing at you."

"A loving mother," she said, smiling. "Now, off with you. Go home and put your feet up. You've had a long, busy day here."

When Deborah had left the store, Bailey replayed in her mind all she had said to her mother.

"And it was spoken with conviction, by gum," she said aloud.

The delivery service would become a reality, and Sweet Fantasy would be a household word. Later there would be a second Sweet Fantasy in another section of the city as her dream expanded to present new challenges.

She would accomplish all she set out to do, step by step, year after determined year. That was how she had gotten where she was now, and that would be the means by which she would go further. The fact that she was in love with William Lansing simply would not be allowed to pull her from the path that—

Her hands flew to her pale cheeks.

Oh, dear heaven, no. No! She was in love with William Lansing? No, absolutely not. She refused to be in love with William, simply wouldn't stand for it.

A wobbly little sob caught in her throat, and tears misted her eyes.

She wanted to flee, run out of the shop, put as much distance as possible between herself and—and what? Between herself and herself? That was what it would take to escape from the truth, and escape was therefore impossible.

There was nowhere to go, nowhere to hide.

The voice of her heart could no longer be ignored.

She was deeply and irrevocably in love with William Lansing.

She shook her head. Well, now what? she asked herself. If William walked through that door in the next second, what would she do? Fling herself into his arms? Slip into her strictly-business mode? Darn it, why didn't she know?

Because all she really knew was that she was terribly confused, and shaken to the depths of her being. All she really knew was that she wanted to wail and weep at full volume. All she really knew was that she loved William Lansing with every breath in her body.

Early the next evening, William tossed a piece of popcorn into the air, tilted his head back and opened his mouth. He frowned as the fluffy snack bounced off his chin.

He was in the family room, and the television was on, showing an old black-and-white movie that he'd lost interest in. The floor was generously dotted with popcorn that had not reached the designated target.

His lack of concentration was due, he knew, to the anticipation of Bailey's arrival at his house. He'd called her in the middle of the afternoon to announce that he had returned to Phoenix earlier than expected.

To his surprise and delight, Bailey had said that she was too busy at that moment at Sweet Fantasy to talk, but could drop by his place after work. He'd agreed to her plan so quickly that the words seemed literally to tumble out of his mouth.

Lord, he'd missed her, he mused. The fact that she'd continually hovered in his mind's eye the entire time he was gone had served to accentuate his driving need to see her, touch her, kiss her, hold her. And he wanted to make love with her with an aching intensity that was like nothing he had ever known.

He glanced at his watch for the umpteenth time, willing time to move faster so that Bailey would be here, in his arms, where she belonged.

Bailey stood in front of William's door and drew a steadying breath. She could, she knew, simply have explained to William on the telephone that afternoon that she would be unable to go out with him tomorrow night due to the late-arriving baskets.

But she had been compelled to see him, to be certain beyond any doubt that she had indeed fallen in love with William Lansing. The very thought of it, of where her raging emotions had taken her, was overwhelming, and terribly frightening.

She felt vulnerable, exposed, cast upon a foreign sea where she'd had no intention of going, powerless to change course.

Unless, she thought, as she knocked on William's door, her imagination had been working overtime, creating a romantic scenario that simply wasn't true. When William opened that door, she'd know, she'd have the answer to all her questions about the depth of her feelings for him.

William turned off the television, then strode to the door and opened it, a wide smile instantly lighting up his face. "Bailey." He stepped back. "Come in, come in."

Bailey felt the color drain from her face as she stared up at William.

Oh, dear heaven, she thought frantically, there was the man she loved with every breath in her body. Yes, she truly loved him, and she was such a befuddled mess, she didn't know what to do.

"Hello? Are you asleep out there?" he said, still smiling.

"What? Oh." She stepped into the entryway, and William closed the door. "Hello, William. I came by to tell you that—"

"Whoa." He held up one hand. "First we have a proper greeting, then we get to the purpose of your visit."

Before Bailey could weigh and measure whether or not it was a good idea, William gathered her into his arms, lowered his head and kissed her.

For the first time in her life, Bailey thought hazily, she was being kissed by and was kissing in return, the man she loved. And it was ecstasy.

The kiss deepened as their tongues met in the sweet darkness of Bailey's mouth. Passions flared with a hot flame, heightening their desire to a burning, aching want and need.

William reluctantly lifted his head, brushed his lips over Bailey's once more, then slowly released her.

"Hello," he said, his voice gritty. "I missed you so damn much."

"Hello," she whispered. She blinked, cleared her throat, then took a step back. "Yes, well, hello, William. I hope I didn't disturb you by announcing that I'd be coming here tonight."

He chuckled. "You disturbed me to the point that I'm about to ravish your body."

"Oh," she said, then laughed in spite of herself.

"Ah, Bailey," William said, his voice gentling. He cradled her face in his hands and looked directly into her eyes. "I'm so glad to see you. I've been thinking about you, missing you, wanting you."

And I love you, Bailey thought.

"Would you like a drink?" he said, dropping his hands to his sides. "Or something to eat? I have popcorn made up."

"No. No, thank you."

"Well, let's not stand here by the door. Come in and sit down." He swept one arm in the direction of the living room.

Bailey preceded him along the entryway and into the living room. She stopped when her gaze fell on a small framed picture on one of the end tables.

"I didn't notice this photograph when I was here before," she said. "It's a lovely snapshot of Alice and Raymond."

She went on around to the front of the sofa and sat down. William joined her, leaving very little distance between them on the cushion. She looked at the picture again.

"Alice and Raymond are delightful together," she said quietly. "There's an aura about them. A person can tell how they feel about each other before they've even spoken. It's hard to explain what I mean, but it's a nearly tangible *something* that radiates from them."

William nodded slowly, his gaze riveted on Bailey as she continued to stare at the photograph. "Yes, now that I stop and think about it, I know exactly what you're talking about, and yes, it is difficult to put into words." He paused, his eyes never leaving Bailey. "It's love, Bailey. That's the bottom line, I think. Alice and Raymond are in love, good, old-fashioned forever-and-ever love."

Bailey shifted her gaze to him, frowning slightly. "My parents were very deeply in love, and I never saw, sensed, what you and I are referring to in regard to Alice and Raymond."

William folded his arms loosely over his chest and squinted at the ceiling.

"I didn't see that much of my folks while I was growing up, but I guess they loved each other, too." He looked at Bailey again. "I took their relationship for granted, because it had always been that way. So maybe we're acutely aware of the special aura surrounding Alice and Raymond because they're of our generation, our contemporaries."

She nodded. "I suppose that makes sense."

"Plus," he went on, pointing one finger in the air, "we, ourselves, are of an age where we're viewing love in terms of the effect it may have on our own lives."

"We are?" She paused. "We are not. I mean, maybe you are, but I'm not sitting around contemplating what it would be like to be in love." She didn't have to contemplate it, because she *was* in love, and it was terrifying. "Besides, I *know* what effect it would have on my life, and it spells *disaster* in big, bold letters."

"Because of your dedication to Sweet Fantasy."

"Yes, which brings me to the subject of why I'm here. I'm not going to be able to keep our date tomorrow night, William."

"Oh?"

Bailey explained the situation with the late-arriving baskets. William had a deep frown on his face by the time she finished her tale.

"That's it," she said. "I'm sorry about our date, but I'm sure you understand why I can't go. As for the wallpapering project with you on Sunday, I didn't have a chance to tell you when you called from the airport that I was meeting the Chamberlains' son at the store on Sunday. So, with that appointment, plus the snafu with the baskets, I won't have a moment to spare."

"What about your employees? If they pitched in, wouldn't that solve the problem?"

"Everyone has other plans. Besides, it's my responsibility to see emergencies through to their proper end."

"That's true, but only to a point. As the owner of Sweet Fantasy, you have the option of delegating tasks, you know."

"William," she said with a sigh, "I don't want to debate this issue. I just felt that, since I knew I couldn't go tomorrow night, I should stop by here and tell you."

"Yeah, okay," he said quietly. "But I still think that you—"

Before William could speak further, a sudden, strange noise interrupted him, the sound coming from somewhere down the dark hall off the living room. He lunged to his feet and stared with wide eyes at the hallway.

Bailey glanced quickly at the hallway, then redirected her attention to William, a questioning expression on her face.

"William?" she said. "What on earth is that noise? If I didn't know better, I'd think it was a baby fussing." She paused. "Now it sounds like a baby who is crying to beat the band."

"It is," he said, still staring at the hallway. "Oh, man, now what? They said he'd sleep straight through until morning. I checked on him a few minutes before you got here, and he was snoring like a lumberjack."

Bailey got to her feet. "You really do have a baby here?"

William switched his gaze from the hallway to Bailey. "Yes. See, there's a young couple who lived in the apartment next to mine before I moved here. They have Christopher—that's the baby. He's six or seven months old. He's a cute little kid.

"Anyway, they were in a real bind tonight. They had special plans to celebrate their anniversary, and their sitter got sick. Everyone else they called was busy, so I agreed to have Christopher spend the night, since I knew I could see you because you were coming here. They put him to sleep in his playpen, and said I wouldn't hear a peep out of him until morning."

"He's peeping," Bailey said, glancing toward the hallway again.

"He's yelling loud enough to crack the plaster, that's what he's doing. I was planning to read books on parenting, how to tend to a baby from day one on, all that stuff. I just hadn't gotten to that project yet." He dragged one hand through his hair. "Well, here goes nothing." He strode across the room and disappeared down the hall.

A baby? Bailey thought incredulously. Great big macho William Lansing was taking care of a baby? Oh, wasn't that the sweetest thing? Little Christopher, however, didn't sound as though he thought it was a terrific idea.

A few minutes later, the baby's wailing grew louder and was accompanied by William singing off key and at full volume.

"You gotta get off the table, Mabel," William belted out as he reentered the living room. "the money's for the beer."

"William Lansing," Bailey yelled, to be heard above the duet, "you can't sing bawdy bar songs to an innocent baby."

"Oh," he said, jiggling Christopher. "Sorry."

The baby had blond hair and tear-filled eyes, was clad in cotton pajamas and possessed the lungs of a linebacker.

"Did you change his diaper?" Bailey asked.

"Yes," William said. He began to walk around the living room with Christopher in his arms. "That was a cinch. You just tape those son of a guns on like you're wrapping a package to be mailed. Hey, Chris, want me to ship you to Hong Kong? Good idea. Lord, why is this kid screaming? Could you help me out here a bit, Bailey? What's wrong with him?"

"You're asking *me?*" she said, splaying one hand on her chest. "I don't remember receiving the Mother of the Year Award. All I know about babies is that they're cute and small."

"Oh, great," he said with a moan. "I thought women just automatically knew this stuff."

"No, William, it doesn't come naturally to the entire female gender, whether they happen to be old-fashioned or not."

"Ah, damn. Well, think about it for a minute, will you? He came equipped with all kinds of junk in a diaper bag. Christopher, my little man, want to hear my old school fight song?"

"Oh, good grief," Bailey said, rolling her eyes heavenward.

"Hip, hip, hooray, here we go to play," William sang at full volume. He continued to march back and forth across the large room, rocking the crying Christopher in his arms. "We're going to win, we'll do it again. Hip, hip, hooray."

He took a deep breath.

"Oh-h-h, hip, hip, hooray, here we go—"

"Cut!" Bailey yelled, slicing one hand through the air. William stopped singing and marching. Christopher wailed on. "Christopher is obviously not at all impressed with your singing."

"He hates my singing. Well, actually, everyone hates my singing."

"William, give him to me, then go look in his diaper bag and see if there's a bottle of juice or something."

"You're on," he said, shoving Christopher into Bailey's arms. He hurried from the room.

Bailey sat down on the sofa and smiled at the crying baby. "Oh, Christopher, you're so sad. What's the matter, sweetheart?" She kissed him on the forehead and inhaled his wonderful aroma of soap and powder. "Hush, hush..."

William reappeared with a bottle of juice. Christopher drew a shuddering breath as Bailey took the bottle from William.

"Everything is all right, Christopher," Bailey crooned. "You've just worn yourself out with this crying, so now it's sleepy-bye time. Here we go. What a nice drink for such a special boy!"

Christopher wrapped his chubby little hands around the bottle and popped the nipple into his mouth. His gaze was riveted on Bailey's face as he sucked eagerly. She shifted him to a more comfortable position in her arms, and blissful silence fell over the room.

"Hey," William said, splaying his hands on his jean-clad hips, "what's your secret, Bailey?" Well, that was easily answered.... Christopher was no fool. He knew heaven when he was experiencing it, and being in Bailey Crandell's arms was most definitely heaven. "What's the magic formula?"

"I have no idea," she said, smiling up at William. She looked at Christopher again. "Oh, William, he's so precious, so adorable."

William sat down next to her and spread his arms out on the back of the sofa.

"Yes," he said quietly, "he's a cute little guy, isn't he? Look at him go after that juice. He was thirsty, that's all. Why didn't *I* think of that?" He lifted one hand to fiddle with Bailey's silken curls. "You're a natural at tending to a baby."

"Don't be silly. You're making it sound as though I came here straight from a conference with Dr. Spock. I've never taken care of a baby before in my life."

"Natural maternal instincts," William said, then nodded. "Yep, that's the answer, and Christopher sensed it. He knew he was finally in the proper hands." He slid a glance to Bailey. "Right?"

Agree, Bailey, William silently directed. If only she'd acknowledge the fact that she had maternal instincts. But no, she'd probably deny from here to Toledo that her hidden maternal instincts had risen to the fore. Bailey wasn't about to agree to *anything* that even hinted at being old-fashioned.

"Well," Bailey said slowly, bringing William from his thoughts, "maybe I *do* have some natural instincts that I haven't been aware of before."

William's head snapped around, and he stared at her with wide eyes.

"Huh?"

Bailey took the now-empty bottle from Christopher and set it on the end table.

"Look, William, he's asleep. He's so beautiful."

"Yes, he's great, except that he snores. Bailey, back up here. Are you saying that you're agreeing with me when I say you have maternal instincts, nurturing instincts?"

Bailey nodded. "Yes, I guess I am."

William opened his mouth to reply, then closed it. He was momentarily too stunned to speak.

He continued to look at Bailey as she smiled warmly, tenderly, at the baby, and for the first time he became totally aware of the enchanting picture she presented as she sat nestling Christopher in her arms.

Oh, Lord, he thought, what an incredible breathtaking sight. It was so lovely, so serene, a woman and child, and with only the slightest stretch of the imagination he could envision Bailey holding *his* child as they sat here together, the three of them, at day's end.

Bailey had just admitted that, yes, she did have natural maternal and nurturing instincts.

Unbelievable. And wonderful.

"Bailey..." he said, his voice low and rumbly.

She turned to look at him. He slid one hand to the nape of her neck, leaned forward and captured her mouth with his. The kiss was searing, urgent, and his tongue delved between her sweetly parted lips to stroke the tongue that eagerly met his.

If Bailey had come this far, perhaps they could go farther.

William broke the kiss as he felt his control slipping, and he took a rough breath before attempting to speak. "What you—" He cleared his throat. "What you just said, Bailey, is sensational. It really means a lot, and it's—"

"Old-fashioned?" she said. She could hear the thread of breathlessness in her voice caused by his bone-melting kiss.

William smiled. "Yes, old-fashioned. It is, you know. It's right on the money." He got to his feet. "I'm going to put Christopher back to bed." He gently lifted the baby from her arms, then brushed his lips over hers before he straightened. "Hold that thought."

Bailey watched as William left the room.

She had, she realized, only a handful of minutes, seconds, to decide whether to go or stay.

If she was standing by the door when William returned, it would be very clear to him that she was leaving.

If she remained there on the sofa with the heat of desire still swirling within her, if she sat there awaiting his kiss and touch, they would make love.

Bailey got to her feet, instantly aware that her legs were trembling. She looked at the door, then back to the hallway where William had disappeared with Christopher. She felt splintered, torn in two, with voices warring in her head, urging her to go, telling her to stay.

William emerged from the dark hall and stopped across the room from her.

"Bailey," he said, his voice hoarse with passion, "I want to make love with you."

The battle in Bailey's mind ceased, with only whispers from her heart remaining.

I love you, William, she mentally declared.

"I want you, too, William," she said softly.

They moved at the same time, meeting in the center of the room, reaching for each other, holding fast.

"There's only the two of us, Bailey." William said. "You." He placed nibbling kisses along the side of her throat. "Me." He outlined her lips with a flicking, tantalizing darting of his tongue. "Together." He kissed each corner of her mouth.

"Yes," she said on a little puff of air, and then his mouth came down hard on hers.

It was ecstasy.

When they had actually moved into the bedroom, Bailey wasn't sure. How their clothes had been removed to lie in disarray on the floor, she didn't know.

All that mattered was William, and the wondrous feel of his hard, naked body pressed close to her soft one on the cool sheets. Hands roamed and lips followed in forays that heightened passions to a fever pitch. Whispered endearments became purrs of pure feminine pleasure and masculine groans of anticipated release.

William paid homage to the soft flesh of Bailey's breasts, suckling, teasing the nipples with his tongue, first one, then the other. His lips moved lower, kissing the velvety softness of her flat stomach, then lower still.

Bailey's hands fluttered restlessly over the taut, slick muscles of William's arms, then across his back, savoring the masculine feel of him, but wanting more, so much more.

She ached from the need of him.

He burned with the want of her.

But still they held back, waiting, waiting, their hearts racing, their breathing rough and labored in the quiet room, their private world.

When the flame of passion threatened to consume them, they joined by unspoken mutual consent, became one in a pounding rhythm.

Worries and woes, fears and confusions, questions and answers, all were forgotten as they once again went to that glittering place of ecstasy they could only soar to together.

Eight

——

Just after lunch the next day, William sat at the desk in the corner of the family room in his house, completing the necessary forms for the business generated during this trip.

He swore under his breath as he realized he'd put information on the wrong line, then tossed the pen onto the file in defeat. He rotated his neck back and forth in an attempt to loosen the painfully tight muscles in his shoulders.

He couldn't concentrate worth a damn, he silently fumed. Never before in his life, *never,* had he allowed what he might be experiencing on a personal plane to interfere with his productivity on a business and professional level.

Even during the past months, as his enthusiasm for his career had dwindled, he'd still mustered maximum effort, due to his pride and the fact that people were trusting him with their hard-earned money.

But that kind of inner control, he thought dryly, was being tested by the appearance of Bailey Crandell in his life.

His Bailey, he mused on. Lord, she was haunting him, taunting him, never totally leaving his thoughts. She was here in his mind's eye, as clearly as though she were standing in front of him. Images of her flitted across his mental vision like an enticing and enchanting movie being presented for him alone.

He could see Bailey smiling, her blue eyes sparkling like a crystal-clear brook on a sunny day. He saw those same expressive eyes flashing with anger, misty with gentleness and warmth, then smoky-blue with desire for him, only for him.

He saw Bailey naked and beautiful, her dewy skin appearing like soft velvet as she lifted her arms to urge him, welcome him, into her embrace and into her body.

Heat coursed through him like hot, rushing lava at the memory of the lovemaking shared with Bailey, and the wondrous beauty of her glowing face and her serene, womanly smile of sated contentment at their sensuous journey's end.

The movie moved on, and he envisioned himself alone in a strange darkness, chilled, turning this way and that as he searched frantically for Bailey.

Then . . . yes . . . a glimmer of light, a bright burst of sunshine that created a circle within the inky darkness. And in the center of the warmth was Bailey, smiling, reaching out for him, beckoning to him to come to her.

He rushed to hold her, and the chill and darkness disappeared. She was half of the whole that made him complete.

And William knew, as he sat in his quiet home, that he was deeply in love with Bailey.

"Oh, man," he said, dragging both hands down his face. He folded his arms over his chest and stared up at the ceiling. "Now what?"

Now he was going to cling to the glimmer of hope he'd felt when Bailey admitted that she did indeed have maternal instincts. He would hold fast to the remembrance of their lovemaking, of how Bailey had given of herself in total abandon.

"I love Bailey Crandell," William said aloud. A slow smile began to replace his frown, then broadened into a wide grin.

He'd waited for a lifetime for this moment, for the realization that he had, at long last, fallen in love. That he and Bailey had a multitude of obstacles in their path would not be allowed to diminish his euphoria.

Bailey Crandell was his.

He would fight the battles necessary to demolish those obstacles, and he would win. Time was on his side, too, as there was still much to do to complete the house, to make it ready to receive The Perfect Wife.

His Bailey.

He smacked the top of the desk with the palm of his hand, got to his feet with a decisive nod and strode across the large room to the door.

At Sweet Fantasy, Bailey found herself constantly looking for the deliveryman who would produce the thirty party baskets. She glanced often at her watch, frowning as precious time ticked away.

Whenever she managed to drag her mind from the basket problem, her thoughts immediately skittered to the image of William.

To add to her frustration, it was an unusually slow Saturday at the store, which meant that Kris would have had even more time than Bailey had anticipated to help with the basket project.

When another half hour went slowly by and the deliveryman still didn't appear, Bailey went into the back room. She sat down at the table and began to review the list of products that would go into each party basket; it was a list she now knew from memory.

She heard, but ignored, the distant tinkling of the bells above the front door, knowing Kris was already greeting any and all who had entered the shop.

When William appeared a moment later in the rear area, Bailey's surprise was evident on her face and in her voice.

"William, I certainly didn't expect you. Would you care to sit down?"

He nodded and crossed the room to settle on the chair opposite her at the table.

William Lansing, Bailey thought, feeling a frisson of heat dance along her spine, then thrum low within her. Last night she'd made love with the man she loved. Now she was once again looking right at him, savoring the sight of every inch of his magnificent, masculine body. Her heart was doing the polka.

"So!" she said, forcing a bright smile. "Did you come to..."

Her voice trailed off as William got slowly to his feet again and started around the table toward her. There was no readable expression on his face, yet there was something intense about him, about the way he moved. Bailey's breath caught and she shivered.

"Come to buy some peppermint candy, or whatever?" she finished weakly.

William stopped in front of her, gripped her upper arms, hauled her to her feet and captured her mouth in a long, breath-stealing kiss.

Bailey, William's mind hummed as heated desire exploded within him. He was kissing, for the first time in his life, the woman he loved, was in love with, would love forever and a day.

As he kissed Bailey, any last, niggling doubts regarding the depth of his feelings for her went up in a poof of passion-induced smoke. He was deeply in love with Bailey.

He slowly, and *very* reluctantly, lifted his head. His gaze met Bailey's, and their eyes mirrored the raging desire within them.

He shifted his hands to frame her face.

"Bailey," he said, his voice gritty. "I love you."

She stiffened, then blinked. "Pardon me?"

"I do, Bailey. I truly do love you." He drew a deep breath, then let it out slowly. "Bailey, I love you with all my heart."

"Oh," she whispered. "Oh, my..."

"I've never said that to anyone before. I'm no expert on this, you understand, but it seems to me that you're supposed to say something in reply to my declaration of love. 'Oh,' and 'Oh, my' really don't cut it. I want—hell, Bailey, I *need*—to know how *you* feel about *me*."

"Oh," she said. "No, forget that. I'm sorry. Just pretend I didn't say 'Oh' again."

Don't you dare, Bailey Crandell, she ordered herself. Do not tell this man that you love him. She'd fallen in love with the wrong man, a man who was seeking a life's partner very different from her. To declare her love for him would only further complicate a situation that was already a disaster.

"Bailey?"

No! "I...I love you, too, William," she heard herself say.

"Ah, Bailey..."

His smoldering eyes visually traced each of her features. When his heated, sensuous gaze lingered an extra moment on her lips, she trembled.

"Say it again," he said. "Please, Bailey?"

"I love you, William Lansing," she said, her voice quivering.

With a groan that rumbled from deep in his chest, he encircled her with his arms and pulled her close, holding her tight.

Bailey rested her head on his chest and heard the wild thudding of his heart, which matched the tempo of her own. She filled her senses with his aroma of after-shave, soap, fresh air and his unique, masculine scent.

At the same time a pulsing heat of desire increased low within her, she felt a strange new peace that touched her very soul.

Like a weary traveler, she mused, she had at long last arrived at her journey's end. She had struggled for so many years to make her way, slowly, step by step, down a path that would lead her to her goals. Where she had made a mistake, she now knew, was in burying the dream of one day loving a special man and having that love returned in kind, sharing a home with him, creating a child.

She'd convinced herself that she couldn't have it all and had accepted that. But now, since William, she knew that Sweet Fantasy just wasn't enough.

Oh, yes, she still had a tremendous sense of pride in what she'd accomplished, and she had no intention of totally turning her back on her business. But there had to be some way to compromise, to make room for everything. Somehow.

William shifted his hands to Bailey's shoulders and eased her away from his aching body. He looked directly into her eyes.

"Bailey," he said, his voice low, "we both know we have some stumbling blocks in our way, but we can solve those problems if we do it together. We'll be determined that the obstacles won't defeat us."

"We'll compromise," she said. "Find a middle road that will work for both of us."

"You bet. But let's not dwell on the heavy stuff right now. Look, I'll get out of here for now so you can work, but tonight we'll celebrate in fine fashion, toast our love, our future, with the best champagne money can buy."

Bailey frowned. "William, I can't go out with you tonight. I already explained all that."

"Well, yes, but things are different now. This is a momentous occasion in our lives, a very big step." He paused. "Couldn't you set the shelf goods out in groups now? Then, when the baskets arrive, you pop the stuff in them, add the perishables Sunday morning, and you're free as a bird tonight."

"That's not efficient. I'd be handling the jars and tins twice when it isn't necessary. Besides, there isn't room here in the back to do that. I have to put things directly into the baskets from the storage shelves. So I have to wait for the basket delivery."

"Group the jars and tins on the floor."

"William, no. It's so much easier just to fill the baskets from the shelves. What you're suggesting is counterproductive."

"What I'm suggesting," he said, his voice rising, "is a way for us to be together tonight, not for an ordinary date, but to acknowledge a major turning point in our lives. It's important, Bailey, a very special event. It's the kind of night that memories are made of. Where's the compromise you just spoke of?"

"Now wait a minute here," she said, anger flashing in her eyes. "If you want to get nitpicky about this, do remember that you just returned from being away for nearly a week because your business demanded your attention. I had no choice but to spend that week alone."

"That man I went to see is an important client. I couldn't just turn my back on him."

"I understand that. Why aren't you extending that same kind of understanding to me?"

"Because you have options, damn it. If you really wanted to go out tonight, you'd pull that candy off the shelves now, counterproductive or not."

Bailey stepped back, forcing William to drop his hands from her shoulders. She planted her fists on her hips and narrowed her eyes.

"You just hold it right there, mister. This is *my* business, William Lansing. I don't tell you how to run Lansing Investments, but you certainly have plenty to say about the operation of Sweet Fantasy."

"Come on, Bailey," he said, dragging a hand through his hair. "That's not fair, and you know it. I'm not telling you how to manage your business, I'm concentrating on the issue of us. That's first for me. Where in the hell is your willingness to compromise? You don't seem to be prepared to give an inch."

"That's not true. The compromise in this case should be in the fact that we both realize that you had to be away all week and realize that we simply can't go out to dinner tonight. When we *can* go, we'll make it our special celebration."

"Second behind Sweet Fantasy."

"Oh, you're an infuriating man!" She folded her arms over her breasts and lifted her chin.

"Bailey, I had no choice in the matter of being out of town. You, however, *do* have a choice. You *could* free up those hours tonight."

"No," she said stiffly. "You're not being reasonable. You're asking me to double my work time by plunking jars of sour balls on the floor this afternoon. That's ridiculous, and I'm *not* going to do it."

"So where in the hell is all this great, wonderful compromise you were talking about?"

"You'd do well, Mr. Lansing," she said with an indignant sniff, "to ask *yourself* that question. You keep throwing it at me as though if there's going to be any compromise, it will be up to me to do it. Well, guess what—that's not how it works."

"Oh, this is just terrific," he said. He began to pace back and forth with heavy steps. "I'm in love for the first time in my life. I've declared that love and been told that I'm loved in return. And then? I'm taking part in a wing-ding of an argument."

He stopped his trek to glare at her.

"Do you know what's missing here?" he said, none too quietly. "Old-fashioned romance. We're supposed to be smack-dab in the middle of moonlight and roses, champagne and raspberries."

"Strawberries. A romantic interlude calls for champagne and *strawberries.*"

"Well, whatever. You get my point. You're the one who is keeping the romantic interlude from taking place."

"Oh, William, shut up. I don't feel like going over and over this another dozen times."

William glared at her. "Fine. I'll shut up. I'll also get out of here before I blow a gasket." He turned and started toward the door. "I'm leaving now, Bailey, but this discussion isn't finished." He looked back at her over his shoulder. "Not even close." He left the room.

Bailey took one step in the direction William had gone, his name a breath away from spilling from her lips. She stopped, sighed, then turned to sink onto one of the chairs at the table, willing herself not to give way to the tears she could feel burning at the back of her eyes.

William Lansing was in love with her. The man she loved returned that love in kind. Marvelous. Fantastic. Except that it was neither marvelous, nor fantastic, because within minutes of their mutual declarations of love, they'd run smack-dab into a brick wall over the subject of compromise.

Should she have agreed to William's plan to enable her to be with him tonight? No. It wasn't compromise, it was her doubling her work load. The compromise would have come in the form of agreeing to celebrate together on another night. Why couldn't William see that?

Smile, Bailey, she told herself as she started toward the front of the store. Oh, forget it. There was no possible way to produce a smile bright enough to chase away the dark, gloomy cloud hovering over her.

And where in the world was the deliveryman with the baskets? Every minute that passed was one less jar of sour balls safely placed in a party basket. At this rate, the entire day was being wasted, which could result in her working the entire night.

Finally, at four-thirty, the truck arrived with a frustrated driver who had suffered through not one, but two, flat tires along his route.

Bailey signed the invoice and managed to assure the man pleasantly that it wasn't his fault. "Goodbye," she said, smiling brightly as the man went out the rear door. "Oh, merciful saints!" she said in the next instant as she glanced around.

She sank onto one of the chairs at the table and stared at the thirty baskets.

They looked, she decided glumly, like thirty thousand. To make matters worse, she was bone-weary, exhausted. She now faced hours of work, when what she really wanted to do was go home, crawl into bed and sleep.

"If there's no rest for the wicked, Bailey Crandell," she said aloud to no one, "then you must be a really rotten person."

At closing time, Bailey shooed Kris out of the door, knowing that she was due to attend an anniversary party for her boyfriend's parents.

"Go, go," Bailey said, flapping her hands. "I'll whip those baskets into shape in no time. Have fun at the anniversary bash."

Kris left, and Bailey turned back to her task.

At seven o'clock, Bailey set another basket in the slowly growing row on the floor, then pressed her fists into her aching back. She yawned, pushed aside a mental vision of a great big bed with a soft, beckoning pillow, and picked up an empty basket.

A heavy knock sounded at the back door.

"Aaak!" she yelled, flipping the basket high into the air.

Her heart was pounding, and her eyes widened when the knock was repeated. She made her way carefully through the maze of baskets to arrive at the door.

"Who is it?" she said, pressing one hand to her forehead.

"William," came the rather muffled reply.

William, she mused. William? Why was William Lansing beating on her door? If that so-and-so thought he could show up there and convince her to walk away from her responsibilities, he was in for a shock—and a piece of her mind. She had no intention of guzzling champagne and chomping on raspberries, or strawberries, or anything else, for that matter.

She unlocked the door and yanked it open.

"Listen, mister," she said, narrowing her eyes, "you've got a lot of nerve coming here to—"

"Help," William said quietly.

Bailey opened her mouth, closed it, then tried again.

"You're going to help me?" she said. "You're here to pack sour balls?"

William nodded, his expression unreadable. "May I come in?"

"Oh, yes, of course."

Bailey stepped out of the way, and William walked into the room. Her gaze flickered over his magnificent physique, which was displayed to perfection by faded jeans and a black knit shirt.

She closed and locked the door, then turned to find William standing so near that she thudded back against the door in surprise.

William moved even closer, bracing one hand flat on the door on either side of Bailey's head. His body was only inches from hers, tantalizing, teasing, causing her to yearn to lean forward, to erase that minuscule distance and feel the hard, strong contours of his body against hers.

But she didn't move. Her palms were on the door, her eyes were riveted on William's, and her heart was beating a wild tattoo. The heated desire churning within her caused a flush to stain her cheeks.

"Bailey," William said, "I love you."

Then he lowered his head and kissed her.

Oh, yes, Bailey thought, and she loved him, so very, very much. She parted her lips to receive William's questing tongue and encircled his neck with her hands. He wove his fingers through her silky curls, and at last, *at last,* pressed his body to hers.

A soft purr of pure feminine pleasure whispered from Bailey's throat. A male groan of need rumbled in William's chest.

The kiss was fire, burning hotter with every beat of their racing hearts.

The kiss was searing, hungry, evoking vivid mental visions of lovemaking shared.

The kiss was ecstasy.

William lifted his head a fraction of an inch and drew a sharp breath.

"Sour balls," he said, his voice thick with passion. "We've got..." He brushed his lips over Bailey's. She shivered. "... to pack..." He traced the outline of her mouth with the tip of his tongue. Bailey trembled. "... sour balls."

"Hmm?" she said, bemused.

William eased himself slowly and reluctantly away from her, ordering his body back under his command, ignoring the ache low within him.

"I'm here to help you, remember?" he said. He cleared his throat, then smiled. "I'm a powerhouse of a sour-ball packer."

Bailey blinked, took a deep breath, then exhaled in a *whoosh* of air.

"You certainly know how to say hello, Mr. Lansing," she said, hearing the thread of breathlessness still in her voice. She smiled. "I'm so glad to see you, William. I hated the way we parted this afternoon. Your coming here to help is a wonderful compromise."

"Well, it's not exactly—" William stopped speaking and frowned as he dragged a hand through his hair. "What I mean is, Bailey, that I haven't changed my views on the compromise that *should* have been made so we could have been together to celebrate tonight."

"Oh, now, wait a minute, William." she said, planting her fists on her hips.

"Whoa!" he said, raising a hand. "Just listen for a second. Okay?"

"Mmm..." she said, glaring at him.

"This isn't the time to cover that issue. Let's just set it aside for now. Going ten rounds on the subject isn't going to get the sour balls packed."

"What, pray tell, are you doing here, if you're not compromising?"

"I'm here," he said, his voice gentling, "because I missed you like hell and wanted to see you, be with you. I couldn't handle the idea that you were here working yourself to death while I was staring at the walls of my house. I'm here because I love you, Bailey."

"Oh." She smiled at him warmly. "Well, I love you, too, William."

"And for tonight, that's all we have to know. Now, Miss Sweet Fantasy, let's get to it. We'll tackle this sour-ball packing and be done in no time. It'll be a piece of cake, you'll see."

"Mmm..."

* * *

At just before 2:00 a.m., William placed a basket on the floor, straightened with a groan and rotated his neck back and forth. He turned to look at Bailey.

"Done," he said. "I swear I didn't know I was lying through my teeth when I said this would be a piece of cake."

Bailey nodded absently, then peered into one of the baskets.

"What are you doing?" William said.

"I want to double-check these. You know, be certain that all the shelf goods that are supposed to be in each basket are in each basket."

"Bailey, give me a break," he said, rolling his eyes heavenward. "We already did that as we went along. Remember?" He paused. "Hey! You! It's two o'clock in the morning, for crying out loud!"

"I know what time it is, William, but I have to be sure there are no mistakes."

"That caps it," he said, throwing up his hands. "That's it. That's all. We're getting the hell out of here. Right now."

Bailey's head snapped up. "William, I always recheck the contents of my specialty baskets for accuracy."

"That's very commendable, *but not at two o'clock in the morning!*"

"Don't you yell at me, William Lansing."

"*I'm not yelling!*" he yelled.

Bailey burst into tears.

"Holy cow," William said as Bailey sank onto a chair. "Now I've done it."

He rushed to her side, began to reach for her, but he stopped when she dropped her face into her hands—and wailed. William froze and stared at her, his eyes wide, his arms stiff and extended, rather like a robot that had suddenly run out of power.

And on Bailey wailed.

Nine

———

"**O**h, man," William said, coming out of his stuck-in-place stupor.

He hunkered down next to Bailey and tentatively placed one hand on her shoulder, the other on her knee.

"Bailey? Why are you crying? Please don't cry. Look, I'm sorry I yelled at you. I *did* holler, I realize that now, and I apologize from the bottom of my heart. No, not just the bottom, my *whole* heart. Okay? Bailey?"

"Just go away," she said, her voice muffled behind her hands. She halted her ear-splitting wailing, sniffled, hiccuped but kept her head bent and her face covered with her hands. "Go."

"Not a chance." He paused. "Are you crying because I yelled? I mean, do you have a thing about yelling that sets you off? Is that the entire cause of your tears? I'm trying to understand, Bailey, I really am. Please talk to me."

She drew a wobbly, shuddering breath, lowered her hands and turned her head to look at him. Tears tracked her pale cheeks, her nose was red, and her lower lip was trembling.

"Ah, sweetheart," William said.

He reached into his back pocket for a neatly folded handkerchief and gave it to her. She dabbed at her nose, and then her hands fell heavily into her lap.

William got to his feet and pulled a chair next to her. He sat down, leaned forward to rest his elbows on his knees and loosely laced his fingers together.

"Let's take it from the top," he said gently. "Was it my yelling at you that triggered this?"

Bailey stared at her hands. "Yes. No." She hiccuped again. "Your reaction was the last straw in a whole stack of straws. I just didn't have any place to put your yelling at me like that."

"I really am sorry. What are the other straws?"

"I don't know... I just... I'm so tired. Even my bones are tired, my teeth, my hair. I'm very tired. I have to work tomorrow... well, today, actually, come back here to the store to fill the chocolate cups with whipped cream so that the Chamberlains' son can pick up the baskets at noon. I never want to see another stupid, ugly basket as long as I live."

"That's fine, but—"

"And furthermore," she went on, as though William hadn't spoken, "do you know how sick a person can get of looking at candy all day long, every day? I really hate sour balls. And fudge. Fudge is gross. Chocolate fudge reminds me of squares of mud. Mud, I tell you. Yucky mud. All I do is work. Work, work, work. It's not enough. I want, I need, more in my life. Are you listening to me, William?"

She stopped speaking, and her hands flew to her cheeks. She stared at William with wide eyes.

"Oh, dear heaven," she said. "I can't believe I just said all that. I sound as though I hate Sweet Fantasy, and that isn't true. You mustn't pay any attention to that blather, William. Please promise me you'll forget it. I'm exhausted, that's all, and got off on a nonsensical tangent that isn't really the way I feel."

"Bailey..."

"I mean, yes, I want more in my existence, but I *do* love my career. It's important to me. Sweet Fantasy is part of who I am. I adore fudge, delicious chocolate fudge. Sour balls are my favorite candy." She jumped to her feet. "I must get home and sleep."

William stood, a frown on his face. "Bailey..."

"I can get a few hours' rest before I need to be back here to finish the baskets."

William gently gripped her shoulders.

"Slow down a minute, Bailey," he said, then kissed her on the forehead. "Okay?"

She nodded, then sniffled.

"Bailey, you know I love you. What I haven't come right out and said, I guess, is that I . . . I want to marry you. Or I want you to marry me. Or however Miss Manners decrees that a guy is supposed to say that. I want you to be my wife, my other half, my partner, the mother of my children."

"Oh," she whispered. "Well . . . Oh."

"Ah, Bailey, it's killing me to see you totally exhausted like this. It's just not right, sweetheart, it really isn't. But because I know you love me, just as I love you, there's a light at the end of this work-work-work tunnel of yours."

"What do you mean?"

"If you'll agree to be my wife, then everything will change. I can't make a commitment to a specific date on the calendar as to when we can be married, because I still have a lot to do to get my house the way I want it to be. But you can hang in there easier, I hope, because down the road, in the future, you *will* reach the end of the work tunnel.

"In the meantime, you can start training people to cover all the aspects of running this place, so that when the baby comes you'll be free to stay home and raise our child. There won't be any more of this packing party baskets at two o'clock in the morning."

"Baby?" she said, shaking her head slightly. "What baby?"

"The one you and I will create when we make beautiful love together. I saw you with Christopher, remember? You're a natural-born mother. You can drop by here once in a while to assure yourself that everything is running smoothly. It will be fine, though, no doubt about it, because you're very intelligent and you'll hire and train the best people available."

"But—"

"So, sweetheart, see this project through, knowing that the time will come when you'll never have to do anything like this again. Fair enough? You bet. Now let's get you home and tucked into bed."

Bailey stepped backward, forcing William to drop his hands from her shoulders.

"I think my tired brain is so fuzzy," she said, "that I'm not understanding what it is you're saying."

He shrugged. "It's very simple."

"Humor me while I run through this. You're asking me to marry you."

"Check."

"However, your commitment to making said marriage a reality hinges on your creating The Perfect House for The Perfect Wife."

"Check."

"Long before I become Bailey Crandell Lansing, I begin to train people to take complete charge of my business."

"Check."

"Following close on the heels of 'I do' is a baby, a little bundle of joy."

"Check."

"I then become an old-fashioned, stay-at-home, bake-cookies-from-scratch mother."

"Check," William said, nodding decisively. "Your brain is still firing on all cylinders. You've got everything right."

She narrowed her eyes. "And you've got everything wrong."

"Huh?"

Anger churned within Bailey, intertwining with her mental and physical fatigue, which was nearly numbing in its intensity. Emotions tumbled through her like an avalanche of heavy boulders, slamming into her, one after the other.

Everything was swirling in a tangled, confusing maze, and as she began to speak she realized that her words seemed to be coming of their own volition from an unknown source. It was as though she were standing outside herself, in a fog, watching and listening to another woman.

"You're wrong, William Lansing," she heard herself say. "I have no intention of giving up any part of Sweet Fantasy, not even for five minutes. This *business* is my baby. I gave birth to it, nurtured it, made sacrifices to assure that it would grow and prosper."

She took a deep breath, then planted tightly curled fists on her hips.

"Listen to yourself, William. You believe you want a wife and family, but I really question whether you're actually ready to make that kind of lifelong commitment. You can't get married until all the wallpaper is hung? Until the swimming pool is built, and heaven only knows what else?

"You're playing mind games with yourself. Can't you see that? Everything has to be perfect, and that's not how life is. You're trying to reprogram me, as though I'm a brainless machine whose buttons you can push as you see fit. That is *not* going to happen. I'm in charge of me, I decide what I will, or will not, do."

She shook her head.

"I don't want to bake cookies from scratch. I don't even like cookies made from scratch. I like store-bought cookies that taste like sawdust. *I am not old-fashioned.* Do you understand that yet? I'm a career woman of the nineties, mister."

"What about compromise?" William said, matching her extremely loud volume.

"What about it? Compromise to you means that I do everything your way. Well, forget it. Just forget it. You claim to love me. Fine. Then accept me the way I am."

"No! Damn it, no! Let me tell you something, Bailey. I literally grew up without a mother, because she continually put her career before her children. Her promises to stay at home just as soon as possible were false and empty—they never came to be.

"She wasn't there when Alice and I needed her, when we were sick, or hurt, or it was our birthdays, or we were in a school play. We were never first with her, important enough to take precedence over her job."

William dragged both hands down his face, then looked at Bailey again.

"It may not sound like a big deal to you," he said, his voice strangely raspy. "I guess it doesn't, because you have a career that is more important to you than...than anything, or anyone, else.''

He drew a shuddering breath.

Bailey stared at him with wide eyes.

"Years and years ago," he went on, "I made up my mind that no child of mine would ever grow up the way I did. My wife, the mother of my children, would be there when they needed her. Old-fashioned thinking? I suppose. But I'll be damned if one of my babies will ever be lonely, crying for a mother who isn't there because her career is all and everything to her."

He stopped speaking and looked directly into Bailey's eyes. Her breath caught when she saw the pain flicker across his face and settle in the depths of his expressive gray eyes.

"I thought," he said, his voice very low, very quiet, "I thought that if we compromised this would all be smoothed over. But it isn't going to work, I can see that now. I love you, Bailey. God, I—" His words were nearly choked off by emotions that threatened to overwhelm him. "I love you so damned much."

"William..."

"We're not going to make it, Bailey, you and I. I guess it's better to find that out now, before we go any further."

William stopped speaking as his throat tightened. He lifted one hand as though to reach for her, then dropped it back to his side. He shook his head, then turned and strode to the door, flipping the lock. After yanking the door open, he hesitated, then stopped, looking back at her over his shoulder.

"Goodbye, Bailey." His voice was hushed, tired, and sounded very, very sad.

And then he was gone, the quiet click of the door seeming like an explosion of noise, causing Bailey to flinch.

"William?" she said. A sob caught in her throat, and tears flowed unchecked down her cheeks. "Oh, William . . ."

She moved on trembling legs to sink onto one of the chairs at the table.

This was a nightmare, she told herself frantically. Dear heaven, what had she done? Horrible words had poured from her mouth like a raging river out of control. In a short span of time, there had been two Bailey Crandells.

When she'd been wailing her head off, she'd been declaring in no uncertain terms that she wanted more than just Sweet Fantasy, needed more, wanted William.

And then?

Merciful saints, she'd gone off the deep end. She'd screamed in William's face that the store was her baby, and he could take a flying leap with his proposal of marriage that came with a clause titled Motherhood.

On the very first day she'd met William, he'd told her about his childhood. She'd listened, but she hadn't *heard* what he was saying. He was striving for perfection now because of the pain, the loneliness, the sense of betrayal, he'd experienced when he was a boy.

We're not going to make it, Bailey, you and I.

"Oh, William."

Tears streamed unnoticed down her face and along her neck. Pressing trembling fingertips to her lips, she stared at the door, willing it to open, knowing it wouldn't. William was gone. She got wearily to her feet and dashed the tears from her face.

Sleep. She had to rest, if only for a few short hours. But once the baskets for the Chamberlains were completed, she was going to concentrate totally on William. Love *would* conquer all, darn it.

And oh, yes, she was definitely, irrevocably, forever and ever, in love with William.

But how on earth, she wondered in the next moment, was she going to convince William that they *could* have a wonderful future? There *was* a compromise for them, a middle road, there just had to be. They could solve their problems if they did it together. She didn't have the answers now, but she believed with all her heart that they were there to be found.

But how could she make William see that their forever was still within reach?

How?

She just didn't know.

Ten

Alice Lansing Wilson marched into William's office, planted her hands flat on his desk, leaned forward and glared at him.

"What is your problem, Mr. Lansing?" she said. "I came by to see if you wanted to have lunch with me and discovered that your secretary—poor, dear, sweet Betty—is plotting your death. She really is, William. She's trying to figure out how to murder you without the police knowing she was the one who did it. I've heard of Monday blues, but this is ridiculous. You're a giant-economy-size grouch."

"Tough," William said. He slammed a drawer of his desk closed to emphasize his frame of mind.

Alice straightened, crossed her arms firmly over her breasts and narrowed her eyes as she studied her glowering brother.

"It must be woman trouble," she said. "Hopefully the woman is Bailey. Tell me, William, is there trouble in Sweet Fantasy Land? You look as though you haven't slept well, and heaven knows you're in a bad mood. Speak."

"Alice, go away."

"No."

"I didn't think so." William sighed. "Yes, all right, it's woman trouble, the woman *is* Bailey, and it's a mess, Alice. It's a king-size, royal mess. Damn it!" he said, smacking the top of the desk with the palm of one hand. "Alice, I love that woman, and I am a very miserable man."

A smile lit up Alice's face. "You're in love with Bailey Crandell? That's fantastic, absolutely marvelous! Wait until I tell Raymond. He was getting a tad annoyed with me for playing matchmaker, but I told him that there are times when a little nudge does wonders. William Lansing is in love. Isn't that something? I'm just so happy for you, sweetheart, I really am."

"Alice, look at this face. Is this happiness in its purest form? Not even close. Did you hear me say it's a mess, a royal mess? Are you paying attention?"

"Goodness, you really are stressed. Spell it out for me, little brother. What's the major malfunction in your relationship with Bailey?"

William lunged to his feet and flung out his arms.

"Bailey Crandell," he bellowed, "likes cookies that taste like sawdust!"

"Oh, good Lord," Alice whispered, her eyes as big as saucers. "You've flipped your switch."

A long, dreary week later, Bailey wandered aimlessly through a department store, not really seeing the merchandise displayed.

After closing Sweet Fantasy for the night, she'd been unable to face another lonely evening in her apartment that she knew would end with a tossing-and-turning night in her bed. When she dozed, she dreamed of William. When she was awake, she thought of William.

She missed him so much. She'd relived that last scene with him in the back room of Sweet Fantasy over and over in her mind and was no closer to a solution, to a compromise, that she could present to William as proof that their problems could be solved.

There was also, she knew, the question of just what the word *compromise* meant to William. It did, indeed, seem that to him compromise represented Bailey totally revamping her life, her way of thinking, her goals, everything. His half of that scenario would be to pat her on the head and tell her that she was a good girl.

"Mmm..." she said, pursing her lips and narrowing her eyes.

She loved William, wanted to marry him, have his baby. Yet she couldn't walk away from Sweet Fantasy, turn it over to others to run, pretend it was little more than a hobby for her. Sweet Fantasy was a part of who she was, just as being William's wife and the mother of his child would be.

Why couldn't William understand that? Why couldn't he let go of the ghosts of his past and compromise?

Bailey sighed, then frowned when she realized that she was standing in front of the display of rainbow-colored towels where she had shopped with William.

A soft smile touched her lips as she remembered how excited William had been about choosing accessories for his dream home. His enthusiasm for everything regarding the house was so endearing, so lovable.

He was an unusual, intriguing, sensitive man who would give a whole new meaning to the age-old adage about a man's home being his castle. The pure joy that emanated from him as he moved through the rooms of his house was wonderful to witness.

With another sigh, Bailey turned away from the display of lush towels and started to walk slowly away. Suddenly she stopped, stiffened, then spun around to stare at the linens again, her mind racing.

"What if—?" she whispered.

She took a deep breath, closed her eyes for a long prayer-filled moment, then hurried toward the exit.

Bailey turned off the ignition and got out of the car, ignoring the butterflies in her stomach and the trembling of her knees. She'd driven above the speed limit after leaving the department store, and she was *not* going to lose her nerve now.

Her entire future happiness would be determined by what took place within the next few minutes, she realized, splaying one hand on her stomach.

As the fact hammered in her mind, she could feel the familiar dark cloud taking shape above her.

"Go away," she said, looking up. "Shoo."

She squared her shoulders, lifted her chin and walked to the door in front of her. She raised a fist to knock, but the door opened before her knuckles could connect with the wood.

And standing before her, all in his magnificent, masculine glory, was William Lansing.

"Bailey," he said, shock evident on his face. There she was, and oh, damn, how he'd missed her. The minutes, hours, days...and nights...since he'd last seen her had been agony.

"Hello, William," she said. *I love you, William.* "You're obviously on your way out." She glanced at the brown grocery bag he held in one arm. "I should have telephoned first, I guess, but it was so important to me that I come. I won't keep you long."

Keep me forever! William mentally hollered.

"I was on my way to your apartment, Bailey."

"You were? Why?"

"Well... No, wait. Why are you here?"

"William, may I come in? Could we sit down and talk, please?"

William nodded and stepped back to allow Bailey to enter the house. They went into the living room, where

Bailey sat on the sofa and William in a chair opposite her. He set the grocery bag on the floor next to him.

Their eyes met and held, and silent seconds ticked by. Each yearned, ached, to rush into the other's arms, but neither moved.

"Why were you going to my apartment, William?" Bailey finally said.

He sighed. "I couldn't stand another night without seeing you, Bailey. I wish I could say that I have a magic solution to our problems, but I don't. I was bringing you this sack of stuff as my way of saying that I respect your right to feel as you do. That our views don't match is sad, incredibly sad, but I don't know how to fix things."

"What's in the sack?"

"Cookies. Store-bought cookies." He managed to produce a small smile. "A wide variety of cookies that taste like sawdust."

"Oh," Bailey said, then stopped speaking as tears misted her eyes.

"Bailey, I want to tell you something. I thought about what you said that night in Sweet Fantasy, about my playing mind games regarding commitment. You were right. I want a wife, family, I truly do, but there was a portion of me that was scared to death that no matter how hard I tried it would all fall apart, be a farce, a hoax, not even remotely close to what I'd dreamed about.

"I guess I had such painful memories of my child-hood that I was afraid history would somehow repeat itself. If I didn't take the final step, actually get married, that couldn't happen. I have that part straight within myself now, and I have you to thank for that."

"But," she said quietly, "you *did* feel that history was repeating itself when I said that Sweet Fantasy was my baby, that I refused to give it up for a husband, a child."

"I... Yes. Oh, Bailey, I love you so damned much. I'd give anything to wave a wand and produce a solution to this mess. I want to marry you, spend the rest of my life with you, but that isn't going to happen, because we're just too far apart on what we want. It doesn't make one of us right, the other wrong. There's no judgment to pass, or blame to place. It just means that you and I are not meant to be together. I hate that, Bailey. God knows I hate that, but..." He shook his head.

Bailey lifted her chin another inch. "William," she said, silently cheering at the realization that her voice was strong and steady, "I believe that I have a solution to our problems, a compromise, a middle road for us."

He leaned forward in his chair. "What is it?"

She clasped her hands tightly in her lap. "Let's confirm a few things first. You built this house, this dream house of yours, for a family. It would be transformed into a home by the addition of a wife, then a child. Right?"

"Check."

"Old-fashioned values would be in operation here, such as made-from-scratch cookies, chitchats after school, the whole nine yards. These would be produced by The Perfect Wife.''

"Check.''

"William, I want to be your wife, but I'm not perfect. In fact, I'm not even close to having, nor do I have the desire to have, the attributes you see in your mind's eye as being necessary for that role. I also want to have your baby, a child created by our love. But, William, to sacrifice Sweet Fantasy to enable me to have those roles would make me less than who I need to be in order to be fulfilled as a complete woman.''

"I know, Bailey," he said wearily. "Why are we going through this again? It's hard enough to have to think about it every waking hour without hashing it over verbally, too. I thought you said you had a solution to propose. Old news is not a solution.''

"I do have a proposal. William, are you basically bored with being an investment broker?''

"Yes, but what does that have to do—''

"Sir, I have the floor.''

"Check," he said, rolling his eyes heavenward. "Carry on.''

"Am I correct in assuming that the joy, the enthusiasm, I observed as you shopped for accessories for this house, cooked, made plans for future projects, was genuine?''

"Check.''

"Then, William, here in this room at this very moment, is The Perfect Wife.''

"You've lost me," he said, shaking his head. "This is sounding more and more like a riddle that I don't understand."

Bailey smiled. "William Lansing, The Perfect Wife...is you!"

"What?"

"Don't you see?" She got to her feet. "Oh, William, please don't reject this out of hand. Listen, okay? Please, just listen and hear me out. You would still be in charge of Lansing Investments, working only as many hours a week as you wanted to. But your real career would be here, in this home, providing the loving, old-fashioned atmosphere that you've dreamed about for so many years. *You'd* be here when our children came home from school, waiting to hear about their day, sitting with them as they eat the made-from-scratch cookies that *you* had baked.

"I would lock the door of Sweet Fantasy at day's end, fulfilled as a career woman who has not been asked to give up what she's worked hard for. I would leave Sweet Fantasy behind each night and come home ready to be a part of our wonderful family."

"Bailey..."

"Oh, William, it would work, it truly would. We can have it all, both of us."

"Bailey..." William got to his feet.

Tears spilled onto Bailey's cheeks. "I love you so much. I don't want to go through the rest of my life without you, William. Will you think about this plan, this compromise?"

"No."

Pain rocketed through Bailey, and she closed her eyes in a futile attempt to stop the tears that poured unchecked down her face.

"No, Bailey, I don't have to think about it," William said quietly, "because I've already made up my mind. Look at me. Please, open your eyes and look at me."

Bailey did as he asked, a sob catching in her throat.

"Bailey Crandell, I accept your compromise proposal, on the condition that you accept my proposal of marriage. Will you marry me? Will you be my partner in life, love, in compromise, until death parts us? Will you eat cookies with me? Yours will be store-bought, mine will be made-from-scratch by me while I'm performing my role of... well, of The Perfect Wife. I like that title, by damn."

"Oh, William," she said, smiling through her tears.

"Say it, Bailey. Say that you'll marry me."

"I will," she whispered.

William stepped forward, framed her face in his hands and gently, so gently, kissed her, sealing their commitment for all time. When he finally lifted his head, love shone in tear-filled eyes of blue and eyes of gray.

"I want to make love with you, Bailey," he said, his voice raspy with emotion.

"Yes. We'll make love, sweet, old-fashioned love-making love until dawn."

With matching smiles they walked from the room toward the master bedroom, eager to close the door on the world. Once there, they quickly shed their clothing, then William threw back the blankets on the bed. He turned to Bailey, his heated gaze sweeping over her, visually caressing every inch of her.

Bailey trembled as her desire heightened, her skin tingling from William's sensual scrutiny. She stood proudly before him, offering to him all that she was as a woman.

He was so magnificent, she mused, so strong, yet so gentle, as perfectly proportioned as a statue, yet real, gloriously real. The anticipation of what they were about to share brought a warm flush to her cheeks and a pulsing sensation low within her.

William extended one hand toward her, palm up.

"I, William," he said, his voice husky, "take thee, Bailey, as my wife, my other half, my soul mate. Until death and beyond, I will love you with all that I am; heart, mind, body and soul. You are my life."

Bailey placed her hand in his and met his gaze.

"I, Bailey," she whispered, "take thee, William, as my husband, the father of my children, the other half of who I am. I love you, William, more than I can ever begin to tell you."

He gently squeezed her hand, then drew her close, wrapping his arms around her to nestle her to him. She encircled his neck with her arms, and their lips met.

It was a soft, tender kiss, a reverent moment that captured the essence of the vows they'd spoken. From that time forward they would be one, united, standing together, and each tucked away the precious memory in a special place in their hearts.

Then William placed Bailey on the cool sheets and followed her there, claiming her mouth, his tongue delving between her lips. One hand skimmed over her, leaving a heated path as it went.

His lips traveled where his hand had been with tantalizing slowness, his tongue flickering against her soft skin. Her breasts ached and he soothed them.

Bailey sighed with pleasure at the sensations thrumming through her. She splayed her hands on William's back, relishing his strength, the splendor of his taut muscles, the moistness of his skin. She filled her senses, and her passion burned brighter.

William moved lower, kissing her flat stomach, then the very essence of her femininity.

"Oh, William," she said.

She clutched his shoulders and closed her eyes, giving herself up to the wondrous ecstasy that she wished to never end. She felt more alive than ever before, and her heart overflowed with love for William.

He retraced his sensuous journey, his want of Bailey causing sweet pain.

"My love," he murmured.

He entered her and she welcomed him.

They were one.

The rhythm of their bodies was perfectly matched, as was the love in their hearts, and the commitment to forever. Their glittering, shimmering place awaited them, and they burst upon it only seconds apart, calling the name of the other.

And there to greet them was their majestic Pegasus.

"The Crandell-Lansing wedding was absolutely lovely," read a section of the society column of the newspaper. "The old-fashioned theme was carried out to perfection, even down to the detail of the mothers of the bride and groom wearing antique lace dresses.

"The only deviation from the old-fashioned motif was the bride and groom's cake, separate from the four-tiered one that was served to the many guests. The newlywed's cake was far from traditional. It was, in fact, a huge chocolate-chip cookie.

"This reporter wishes Bailey and William Lansing every happiness in their future life together."

* * * * *

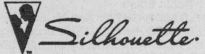

by Ann Major

Take a walk on the wild side with Ann Major's sizzling
stories featuring Honey, Midnight...and Innocence!

IN SEPTEMBER, YOU EXPERIENCED...

WILD HONEY Man of the Month
A clash of wills set the stage for an electrifying romance for
J. K. Cameron and Honey Wyatt.

NOW ENJOY...

WILD MIDNIGHT November 1993
Heat Up Your Winter
A bittersweet reunion turns into a once-in-a-lifetime adventure for
Lacy Douglas and Johnny Midnight.

AND IN FEBRUARY 1994, LOOK FOR...

WILD INNOCENCE Man of the Month
One man's return sets off a startling chain of events for
Innocence Lescuer and Raven Wyatt.

Let your wilder side take over with this exciting series—only from
Silhouette Desire!